9743

F
M Morris, Judy K.
   The crazies and Sam

9743

Date	Borrower's Name	Rm. No.
SEP 18 1987	*Oliver*	3

F
M Morris, Judy K.
   The crazies and Sam

THE CRAZIES & SAM

The Crazies & Sam

a novel by Judy K. Morris

The Viking Press · New York

For Day

First Edition
Copyright © 1983 by Judy K. Morris
All rights reserved
First published in 1983 by The Viking Press
40 West 23rd Street, New York, New York 10010
Published simultaneously in Canada by Penguin Books Canada Limited
Printed in U.S.A.
1 2 3 4 5 87 86 85 84 83

Library of Congress Cataloging in Publication Data
Morris, Judy K. The crazies & Sam.
Summary: A young boy living in Washington, D.C., with
his divorced father tries to come to terms with some of
the contradictions of life and in the process learns
something about love and responsibility.
[1. Fathers and sons—Fiction. 2. Single-parent family—Fiction
3. Washington (D.C.)—Fiction] I. Title.
PZ7.M8283Cr 1983 [Fic] 82-8380
ISBN 0-670-24545-3   AACR2

Contents

1
See Ya, Sam

"Sam," Phillip said, "come hold this pigeon still so I can get it tied."

That crazy guy was trying to tie a rope around the stiff and slippery legs of a dead pigeon. He was trying to do it without touching the pigeon and without smelling the pigeon, probably without even looking at that disgusting pigeon.

Of course, I wasn't going to touch that pigeon, either. I looked around for a stick. Nothing. Nothing up on that roof but Phillip and me and the pigeon. Finally I broke off a small branch from a tree that was hanging over and used that to press the pigeon

1

tight against the roof, while I looked the other way and held my breath. The difference between Phillip and me is I don't pretend to be brave.

I was trying to think how I got into this. Just that morning, when Dad was going over the rules again, he had warned me about Phillip.

Dad and I had been eating our good Saturday morning pancake breakfast and already feeling hot. Our apartment is the whole third floor of a row house, and the windows were open front and back, north and south, over the street and over the alley, but no wind came cooling through. This hot morning, the hot end of our hot summer, the windows let in only more heat, and street sounds—someone calling, car noises, dogs barking, radio music. We were going to go to a nice cool movie when the day got really hot, around two.

"Sam?" I could tell from his voice that Dad was reading off one of his brain lists. He's got a brain pad up there, and a brain pencil, to make his rules and his lists of things to be done. "I'll be giving you your own key again this year, for after school, so I'd like to go over the ground rules. Most important is just don't let anyone in."

"You've told me that a thousand times."

"You can stay here or play outside or come to the office, anytime." Dad's office is just a few blocks away. I like to go there and work their machines. "I'll have work for you, making copies or stuffing envelopes."

2

"For pay?" I had to be careful. They didn't used to pay me.

"For pay. Or you can visit someone after school. Just be sure you let me know if you go to someone's house. I always want to know where you are."

"I know. And don't get into a car with a stranger. I know all that stuff, Dad."

"And no guests when you are alone. Especially Phillip. When Phillip is here, I want to be here, and the fireman, and the policeman, and the ambulance driver...."

I could just see the fireman and the policeman and the ambulance driver sitting around the kitchen table having a cup of coffee with my dad, waiting for Phillip to do something terrible.

"Dad! He's not that bad!" Phillip *is* that bad. Phillip's ideas shift faster than the gears on a racing car, from experiments, to adventures, to real, actual, menacing dangers.

I don't exactly know why Phillip was my friend. Maybe because he'd sat next to me in second grade. He lived a few blocks away, and we could play after school. And his parents were divorced, too, although we didn't talk about that. Phillip was funny and interesting, even if some of his ideas were terrible, and even if sometimes he was mean.

But I would rather go to his house. His mother loved him by buying him lots of candy and stuff. My father loved me, he said, by not letting me have much.

3

So, of course, I loved to go to Phillip's house, and eat.

Dad was still rolling down the rules. "No guests, and call me if you go to someone's house."

"You already said that one. I know them, Dad. I'm really old now."

"You certainly are, Sam. What grade will you be in this year?"

I never knew if he was pretending when he asked me something like that. It scared me to think he really might not know and I would be the only one to remember the important information about me.

"Sixth grade," I said, very softly.

"Samuel J. Diefenbach," he said, "of the strong brown eyes." He leaned back in his chair and stared at me like I was something wonderful. My dad says my eyes are very big and very dark. They just look like eyes to me. His eyes are brown, too, but not so dark as mine. "Samuel J. Diefenbach, of the strong brown eyes, who is about to start sixth grade, who loves his jeans and hates his corduroys, whose hair is always flopping around even when it's just been cut, who biked fourteen miles with his father along the C and O canal this summer and plans to bike even farther this fall, who makes himself grilled cheese sandwiches for breakfast and has the messiest room on the block."

I did sound pretty good. Of course, there were some parts about me that Robbie J. Diefenbach didn't know.

"One other thing, Sam." His brain pencil checked off another item on the Saturday list. The other thing, of course, was I had to clean up my room.

And, of course, he had to work. Robbie often worked on Saturdays, sometimes at his office, sometimes at home. While he worked, until time for the movie, I was going to have to clean my room and take care of myself, which is why I thought of calling Phillip.

Most Saturdays Phillip's father came to get him at noon. Now, when I called, Phillip said he could come for only fifteen minutes. His mother wanted him back by ten-thirty to go to the park. She said his father would take him to movies all weekend, so they had to go get some nice fresh air together before he left. His father, his mother, that situation.

"I guess fifteen minutes of Phillip is worth a couple of hours of anyone else," Dad said.

I started picking up the things in my room. No point in waiting for Phillip. He wasn't going to be any help.

When Phillip came, he began picking things up, too, picking things up and putting them down, anywhere else, never where they belonged.

He picked up my kite. "Hey! Let's go fly it."

"I have to clean up my room before I can go out."

"We don't have to go out. We can fly it from the roof."

"I'm not supposed to go up there."

"Who would see us?"

5

Oh, brother. "I have to clean my room." When I got back to that, he knew I couldn't think up any more reasons.

"You can do that later," he said, and started out.

Dad's desk is right by the door. He sat with his elbows on the desk, his head between his hands, looking at papers.

"I'll be right back, Dad," I said. "We're just going up to the roof to fly the kite."

Phillip gave me a dirty look before he smiled at Dad. "It's an experiment, Mr. Diefenbach, just like Ben Franklin's." Phillip thinks calling something "an experiment" makes parents more likely to let you do it.

Dad leaned back in his chair and looked at Phillip and me for a very long moment; mostly he looked at Phillip.

"No, I think not. Wise old Ben, boys, kept two feet on solid ground. Besides, Phillip, that experiment's been done. It would be a waste of your valuable time."

Good old Dad.

"But—" said Phillip.

"Phillip, my friend," Dad said, "despite our occasional disagreements, I really do care whether or not you get yourself killed. No."

Any other kid, if his friend's father said no, would give up. Phillip took it as a challenge. He came back in my room, dropped the kite on the floor, and looked around. "Hey!" he said. "These!"

He picked up the bag of cloth loops for weaving pot holders that my grandmother had given me for Christmas. I had made four. One for my dad, and one I sent to my mom, and one I sent to my grandmother, of course, but I couldn't think of who would love to have the fourth one, so I gave that to Dad, too, and then I stopped making them. I had about a thousand loops left.

"You know, if you want," Phillip said, but he was already doing it, "you can make a good rope with these." He showed me how to knot them, one through the other. "Too bad you don't have something good we could lower out the window. Every time your dog needed a walk, we could just walk him from up here. You should have a dog, Sam." Phillip was watching me out of the corner of his eye.

"Good thing I don't have a dog," I said. He would do it.

When Phillip got his next idea, Dad was too deep down in his work to help me. He looked up and smiled at us, as we came by, and Phillip said, "We're just taking the rope out." For a walk, I thought, like a dog? But still my dad smiled back, not listening, and Phillip went out the door. I watched while Dad turned his head back to his work and his smile melted back into his usual face. I couldn't think of anything to warn him about; I didn't know what Phillip planned to do. I shut the door.

The roof was easy to get to, just up a few stairs

and through a door that had an easy bolt. My father had shown me how long ago, in case of fire, but I was not supposed to go there.

The roof was hot under my bare feet. I picked up one foot and then the other, and looked around. Washington, D. C., is a flat city and the buildings are low, so from our roof you can see a long way, all around, over the next street and the next. I can see the National Cathedral on its hill from my roof; some people can see the Capitol, on Capitol Hill, or the Washington Monument, from theirs. The houses are row houses, which touch each other at the sides. Our row of nine houses makes a little island of rooftops in the city air. You can walk onto your neighbor's roof, if you like, if you dare.

Our roof was empty. The interesting things—the solar heaters, the little garden tubs with flowers, the sunbathing chairs—were on other people's roofs. A big tree bent over our house and had dropped a few leaves and twigs. Leaves and twigs were not enough for Phillip.

He bounced the loop rope in his hand and looked carefully around. "There's got to be something. . . ."

He began a slow walk around the roofs near ours. "*There* it is!" he called. He walked toward that dead pigeon as if he had had an appointment with it and it was late.

I had never seen a dead pigeon before, on the roof

or anywhere else, for all the years I had lived in the city and all the thousands of live pigeons I had seen. It looked sick around its dead eyes, and the feathers were rumpled and bent, and one of its legs was crooked. The wings were not neat and tight by its body, but flopping this way or that, whenever Phillip moved the body. Every time the body moved, I thought I could smell it.

The stiff, crooked leg caused Phillip problems in tying on the rope. I had to get the stick and hold it still so Phillip could stand to do what he was doing.

I was sure Phillip's fifteen minutes was up, but he wasn't about to go home. Phillip left only when he wanted to, suddenly, when things got very boring or very bad.

He finished the knots, and then in the same motion he stood up and swung the pigeon around his head. "We're going to *fly* this pigeon!" he said. The wings flopped out in the air a little, but it didn't look like it was flying. It looked dead. Phillip started to run with it, still circling, across the roofs, back to our roof, and toward the front edge.

"Look out!" I yelled.

But he stopped in time. With a huge swirling circle of a throw, he cast the dead pigeon out of sight, over and down in front of our building.

He lay down to look over the edge. I was dizzy, just watching him. But when nothing happened, when

9

all I could see was his arm moving slightly, where it hung over the edge, I knew if I wanted to know anything I would have to look for myself.

"If only I can land him," Phillip said. I got down and started to crawl toward the edge.

Luckily, unluckily, I never saw what happened down below.

I heard a man scream. There was a thump, and then a crash of breaking glass or china. An instant later someone grabbed me by my ankles and jerked me back from the edge. As I sat up, rubbing the undersides of my arms where they had burned in scraping against the hot roof, I saw Phillip sitting, leaning back on his arms, with just the briefest bit of loop-rope showing between his hand and the edge of the roof.

My father was standing behind us, furious.

"I finally realized all that noise and running was you two. Sam, what's gotten into you? You're not supposed to be up here. Phillip, what are you doing with that rope?"

Phillip didn't answer.

"Phillip?"

Slowly, reluctantly, Phillip began to haul in the line. Arm length by arm length, the pile of gaily colored loops curled and grew beside him. It was a long rope. That pigeon must have touched the sidewalk.

I waited anxiously for the end to finally appear,

as if I expected much more than the sagging, raggedy, used-up pigeon, as if I expected the scream and
the crash and the whole disaster that I hadn't seen
to come up over the edge.

Slowly, slowly, Phillip pulled. Dad, mad as he was,
couldn't do anything but wait. But Phillip must have
known. He must have been able to tell, because when
the last little end of the rope flipped up over the edge
of the roof, there was nothing there, not a single
feather.

Robbie had not heard the scream and crash; he
had come out on the roof just a second after that
happened. I don't think he even knew he had missed
something.

"Phillip?" he said. "Weren't you supposed to be
home by now?"

Phillip nodded and grinned. He knew he was home
free. In a businesslike way he coiled the rope into a
neat circle and handed it to me, with the tiniest glance
that said he was right and I was wrong about a thousand things. He went to the door.

"And, Phillip. Phillip! You must never, never come
up here again. It is extremely dangerous."

"Yes, Mr. Diefenbach. Good-bye." And just before
the door shut, there came the lightest, meanest sound,
"See ya, Sam."

That was all for Phillip. But for me, it was no
movie, and back to cleaning my room, and staying

in my room for the rest of the day, thinking about what I had done. Well, he couldn't tell me what to think.

After Robbie said all that, I tried: "That ain't fair, Dad."

" 'Ain't' is a lousy word, Sam."

"Saying 'ain't' feels good when you're mad."

"That's enough, Sam. Let's go on down."

On the way, we heard footsteps on the stairs, and the new man who lived downstairs came running up. I hung onto the railing, hoping I was safe.

"Mr. Diefenbach? I heard you up here, and I just had to tell someone. The most curious thing! A dead pigeon fell out of the sky and landed on my windowsill. Knocked off one of my plants."

"Was anyone hurt?" Dad asked.

"Oh, no. But wasn't that a curious thing, a pigeon falling dead right there? I'd never seen a dead pigeon before, come to think about it."

"Very curious," Robbie said. He looked at me and raised his eyebrows, and we went in.

I hated being caught between Dad and Phillip. My own dad should have known I really didn't want to do those things. He knew I could take care of myself. Probably he was angry because we interrupted his work so much. That stupid guy would rather work than go to a movie. I knew it.

2
Jouncing
Shadows

So there I was in my room, stuck.

The rooms of our apartment were strung out like beads. My room was at the front; next was the living room, which was also Dad's study; then the dining room, which was also his bedroom; and in the back, the little kitchen and the little bathroom next to it, overlooking the alley.

But my room was the biggest. I had shelves and walls to put things on, and boxes and drawers to put things in, and a thousand things to put:

My acorn collection. I didn't know what to do with an acorn collection, so it was just there, being beautiful.

All the stuff I keep from McDonald's, when I ever get to go.

A big pile of postcards from my aunt Kristie. She travels a lot, and she's great on postcards.

My cracked, old aquarium. I had given the mice away, but I hadn't cleaned it out yet.

The big photograph of baby alligators that my mom, Sheila, had sent me from Florida. She took it herself. I could see four alligators hidden in the marshy water, but since I hadn't noticed the fourth one until I'd had the picture for about a week, I always suspected that there might be another one. I had put the picture on the wall over my bed, where the street light shines up through the window. Some nights I would look for alligators in my mom's photograph to keep my mind off scarier things.

My big map of Washington, D.C., with our block marked. I live about exactly north of the Washington Monument.

Also, that boring nutrition poster Dad gave me. I wished I could clean *that* up and throw it out, but I didn't want to insult the guy.

Handcuffs, locked forever. Phillip lost my key.

Clothes all around, of course.

I liked my things, but all jumbled together like that they would make a boring day. I wished I could just push a button and they would clean themselves up. I pushed the light switch. Nothing happened.

Well, the light went on.

I went over to my window. There was nothing down there. The man had swept away all his plant mess. The dead pigeon was in the gutter. Otherwise, everything was the same.

My block is right downtown, but we don't have any of the monuments around here. Sometimes we go see them, but they're mostly for the tourists. Downtown, there's usually something to see because there are all kinds of stores and all kinds of people. But not many children live right around here—mostly grown-ups—and that makes me feel small in the streets sometimes. That's another reason Phillip was my friend.

I was mad at Phillip.

I turned around to start the cleaning. Nothing else to do. But then I heard good sounds coming from the alley—people talking and laughing, the thump of heavy things, metal wheels on concrete, someone calling to a dog. It was the Pickers.

Like a flash, I was out of my room and speeding past Robbie, calling to him that I had to go to the bathroom, speeding to the bathroom, slamming shut the door, and pushing up the window as high as it would go. It was the Pickers, all right.

The Pickers came through the alleys helping themselves to people's trash. They sold stuff; that was their business. Their clothes were old, they looked

15

poor, but they took only the best junk, and they had fun. I loved the Pickers, but I never saw them much, and they didn't know me.

Now they were pushing a big, heavy chair up onto their cart. The two men lifted, and the woman tried to push the cart underneath. A black dog was hanging around, trying to get at something that was squished into the alley bricks under the chair. It must have smelled delicious because the dog wouldn't give up. Four times he came to sniff, and four times one of the men gently pushed him away with the side of his leg. The dog came back again, and the man laughed, and called him by a swear word, and then he moved over to let the dog enjoy a taste and a smell.

I had names for them. The woman, who sang, I called the Singing Picker Woman, and the big man I called the High Picker. The other man I called the Dog Picker. Sometimes there was a dog following that man, and sometimes he was calling for his dog; sometimes it was the same dog, and sometimes it was a new one. There was always something going on about dogs with that man; that's why he was the Dog Picker.

Every time I saw the Pickers, I saw something happen. Once the High Picker lifted a blue bottle from the bottom of a trash can up to the end of his long straight arm high over his head, and let it go. The bottle smashed on the bricks into a thousand blue points, and the three Pickers laughed.

Now the Dog Picker jumped up and sat on the stuffed chair as it rested, tilting, on top of the wagon. He called to the black dog, slapping his knee, trying to coax the dog up.

"That dog's too smart to get up there," the Singing Picker Woman said. "You're going to fall, James, fall and break open your head."

"Push me!" said the Dog Picker.

The Singing Picker Woman pushed on the wagon handles, but nothing happened. "Push him," she said to the High Picker. "Push that fool."

The High Picker pushed. The cart jerked, and the Dog Picker lost his balance and jumped down, laughing wildly, flapping his arms like chicken wings and landing right by the dog. The dog jumped up and licked his face and welcomed the man back down.

"You're some smart dog," the Dog Picker said. "I'm going to keep you."

"Smarter than you, James," the woman said. She and the High Picker laughed.

"Come on," said the High Picker. "We won't get more in that cart. Let's head for home."

I leaned far out the window, watching them out of sight. I wondered where their home was. I wished I had a dog. I wished I could get those Pickers to clean my room with me. I could have some fun with them! I could give them some really good junk.

I went back and looked around my room. The rope

was the only interesting thing, the only thing that was new. If I used that long loop rope, I could make a net ceiling for my room. I could hammer nails all the way around the room, about two feet below the real ceiling. Then I would string the rope back and forth across the room. I knew how perfect it would look. And it would sort of mess my room up again, nicely, a little.

I started putting in the nails. Dad heard the banging and stuck his head in the door. Poor Dad. He has this rule—against him, for once—that my room is my own room and I can do what I want in there. I could see he could hardly stand it, all the nails and the little puddles of plaster dust on the floor. But all he could do was to go away.

When I had the ceiling done, I picked up a little blanket I used to have when I was a baby and bunched it up. When I tossed it, it fit between the ropes going up and then brushed the real ceiling and spread out and caught on several strands of the rope ceiling on the way down. I held my breath as the weight of it hit, but the rope held. The effect was just what I had hoped, a sort of canopy over one part of the room, and a new darkness below.

I tossed up anything that might possibly stay: little pillows, hats, animals, pajamas, a yo-yo, a bamboo cane. My red sweater stayed, and my red, white, and blue tie-dyed thermal underwear. Everything I stuck up there added to the jouncing shadows on the floors and the walls. The Mexican sombrero Kristie brought me made a huge oval shadow, and my jump rope hung down over my bed.

When everything was up, I lay down and gave little jerks to the jump rope to make the ceiling wiggle. I hoped Dad could understand that I had cleaned the room and that this was a new mess.

After a while, watching the shadows, dreaming, I forgot the ceiling was there; the jumping shapes jumped into my mind and made me think of scary things.

At night when I went to bed, I knew there were kidnappers and robbers waiting in my room to get me as soon as I fell asleep. I knew it. Once I told Dad, but he laughed and said, "Hey, that should be one advantage of not having much money. My son doesn't have to worry about being kidnapped. No ransom available! Don't worry, Sam." He just laughed.

I kept my fears to myself after that, but I kept them. How's a kidnapper going to know my father doesn't have enough money?

I decided I could use my beautiful new loop rope ceiling for defense. I could load the net with weapons—a pan of water, carefully balanced, a box full of those jacks I never used, two or three books placed over the windows and the door. I could attach a long string to each bomb so that when I was lying in bed, I could control it all.

I would listen for the smallest sound and keep my

eyes open. I would be ready when he came, my kid-napper. As soon as that man crossed the threshold, he would be bombarded by a thousand weapons: boots, jacks, glue, and salad dressing, light bulbs, forks, shampoo, and a thousand horrible dry soy beans from the health food store. And when I had him to-tally confused, I would pull the master rope and the whole ceiling would fall, like a net, and close him in. And then I would call my dad, and he would call the police.

It was a terrific idea, and it probably wouldn't work. But I lay in the safe daylight and went over the plan, so powerful inside my brain, several times.

By the time Dad called me for supper, I felt a lot better. He did, too. He had finished his work, and we went to the seven-thirty show. We stopped at Sears and bought new, high white sneakers with golden wing stripes for me, a good running kind that cost a little more, and then I was all ready for school to start.

That night my bed did feel safer, for a while, while the light was still on; I kept my jump rope in my hand and jiggled the net a little while I read.

But when my light was off, the street lamp shining in the windows made new, strange, different shad-ows on the wall and on the real ceiling up above. I had to turn away, toward the wall, and watch my mom's alligators so I could go to sleep.

A few days later I took that ceiling down.

3
The Shark in Language Arts

With just one parent living with just one kid, there's more each person has to do. That's why Robbie makes his rules. He thinks if he sets up enough rules we'll be okay. But he's the only one who can change them, and he does change them, and that's not fair. And if I get mad at Dad, there's no Mom to go to for a hug.

About two weeks after school started, we had one of those bad times.

I was up early, working on an important airplane model. I couldn't get the halves of the plane's fuselage to stay glued together; I tried about a thousand ways. Then, when I had only half an hour left to get dressed, eat my breakfast, make my lunch, and get some help from Dad on the model before I went to school, that's when he came busting into my plans. As he walked in, I could almost see his brain pad flipping its pages.

"The timing's going to be a little tight this evening, Sam," he said. "Susan and Whit are coming for supper." Oh, brother, Susan and Whit. "Also, we have to pick up the food from the co-op. Could you get it, right at five-thirty? I'll try to leave work on time and have dinner started by the time you get back."

"Yuk!" I threw down the fuselage parts and went to get my clothes. That's what I meant about my mom; I bet if Sheila lived here, she wouldn't make me pick up the co-op.

I really hated that co-op. All these families and people got together to buy their fruit and vegetables from the wholesale markets. Every Tuesday one family had to shop and another family had to divide the food into twelve bags. Then you had to go pick up your bag at the divider's house and pay six dollars for the next week. You didn't even know until you got home and opened the bag what kind of stuff you'd be stuck eating the whole week long.

Dad said being in the co-op meant you got better food, and more food, for less money, and the chance to meet some interesting people. I said being in the co-op was boring.

Every week the bags of food seemed the same. And

Tuesday night supper was the same, every week. Robbie cooked onions and hamburger with one of the vegetables cut up in it—usually eggplant—and put yogurt on top. He cut up some other vegetable in dressing and called that salad. Fruit, probably with more yogurt, was the dessert. Every Tuesday.

Sometimes we got extra-sweet, super-size strawberries or grapefruit or pineapples, but that didn't make up for the trouble when it was our turn to sort all that stuff into twelve paper bags. Even going to get the bag each week was a pain.

"I'll leave the money here," Dad said, following me into the kitchen. "Thanks, Sam."

"I really hate that co-op, Dad. Do we have to do it because we're so poor?"

"Sam! We're in the co-op because we get better food."

"And it's cheap."

"I don't want you to worry about money. Let me think about that. We're not poor, Sam. We just have to be careful."

And be in the boring co-op.

"Thanks, Sam. They're coming at six-thirty."

I didn't like Susan or Whit; they were co-op people, and there was no more grape jelly for my sandwich, and my fuselage was never going to stay together, and I had crumpled the plastic tip off the lace of one of my new sneakers, pulling too hard, and Susan and Whit were a couple of real fakers and they were going to talk all night, so *bang! slam!* with the peanut butter jar top and punch the toaster lever down.

"Come on, Sam, I need your help. You can eat any of the fruit you like, as soon as you come home."

"Okay," I said, and pressed the deal further. "And can I make myself a grilled cheese if the co-op has eggplant again? I ain't eatin' any eggplant."

"Sure, Sam," he said.

"And, Dad? I need you to help me as soon as you come home. I'm stuck on my model."

"I told you, Sam. We have company tonight. I'll try my best, but if I can't do it in a minute or two, it may have to wait."

"Dad, I need your help so I can work on it tonight, while those guys are talking all night." I liked the firm and truthful way I explained that to him.

"Sam. I will try to help you with the model, but I won't have a lot of time." That, unfortunately, was very reasonable. My father was always reasonable. I hated it when he made his voice so kind when he was saying such unfriendly things.

I hated it when I would rage and cry, flaming crazy. My muscles moved inside my skin, but they had no power to change anything.

Suddenly I was pure yelling mad. I knew it when the "No!" screamed out of my mouth. "No! I won't pick up the stupid co-op!"

Dad's voice got quieter and kinder and firmer. "Yes,

Sam, you will." My voice was screaming, "No! No!"
a thousand times louder than my father's voice, but
I knew his quiet voice would win. He tried to hug
me, but I broke away from him and started stuffing
my mouth with cinnamon toast.

The toast helped, and the juice that Dad poured
for me helped. There was quiet in the kitchen, and
I left.

At school Mrs. White also had a plan for me, also
something I had to do to help someone else. Mrs.
White wasn't a bad teacher; at least she didn't scream
at kids. But this morning, when I needed to be left
alone, she said I had to help the new boy.

That classroom is big and bright and noisy in the
morning when I come from my own quiet house, and
I can never be alone. The high ceiling and the big,
round lights hanging down and the kids calling and
teasing sometimes gave me a headache.

I kicked the broken sliding door of the coat closet
to move it over an inch and stuck my jacket in. Phillip
waved, and I started over. That was when Mrs. White
stopped me.

She told me she would be introducing a new unit
on descriptive writing, and she wanted me to sit by
the new boy and guide him through the class, because he couldn't write. Write? This kid couldn't even
talk. The other new kids had already melted into the
class; this kid was still "the new boy."

"Do your best, Sam. Not knowing English well is a real handicap for him. See if you can get him to write anything at all." Mrs. White smiled. "That should be an interesting educational experience for you."

I went to my desk to get my pencil and paper. Phillip said, "Hey, Sam! Did you know Billy Rugh's father is an alcoholic? And his mother has an artificial leg?"

That news was exactly the kind of educational experience I was interested in, but Mrs. White wouldn't understand. I made a good-bye face to Phillip and walked across the room.

The new boy smiled and said nothing, as usual. That boy wore tan clothes all the time, always very neat. It really bothered me how neat his clothes were; how could he be comfortable? With his tan clothes and his tan skin, his black eyes really shone out. His eyes were bright, and he smiled a lot, but it's hard to get to know a person who won't talk.

He came from some country over by the Pacific Ocean—Burma or Indonesia, one of those. His father worked at the embassy. Mrs. White had shown us his country on the map the first day of school. She had written the boy's long name on the board. The boy had said it softly for us, three times, but no one understood. He didn't talk and he didn't have a name we could use, so no one paid much attention to him.

Mrs. White began to talk about descriptive writing. Once in a while she wrote one of the words she said on the board: "Observation," "Adjectives," "Precision."

I slumped down in my chair and ran my ball-point along the rubber rims on my sneakers.

She started reading some examples.

I hunched myself up in my chair and began to draw. I tried to make a spaceship, but I couldn't get it right.

I looked over at Phillip. He was working furiously over his paper. Probably he was getting his spaceship right. I turned to a clean page and started to draw a jet.

The new boy was watching me. I turned my paper so he could see better. I wasn't getting the jet right, either. I drew some clouds behind. Clouds are easy.

When I looked at the new boy again, I found he had learned something from me, but not what Mrs. White expected. He had learned that you could draw in class.

And what a drawing! While I was still working on the outline of my plane, that kid had a whole war going. His plane had guns blazing out the front, jet fire blazing out the back, a big, strong pilot, smoke everywhere, and the sky all around filled with falling planes. It was beautiful.

The new boy was grinning at me. He pointed to the pilot and pointed to me. It was sort of embarrassing. I shook my head.

Also, I was embarrassed about teaching that boy to draw in class. I didn't want to get the poor kid in trouble.

I took a clean piece of paper and wrote "Sam Diefenbach" in the upper right-hand corner. I pointed to myself and whispered, "My name," then pointed to the name on the paper, to myself, to my name. Then I got him a clean paper and pointed to the same corner on his paper. "Your name," I said. He smiled. He really didn't like to talk. I gave him his pencil and pointed to the paper again.

He wrote his long, impossible name. The boy's writing was clear and neat, but I couldn't read it. I could read a "K" at the beginning and an "e" at the end, but everything in between was loops and lines. I felt stupid not being able to read such neat writing. I tried to pronounce it. The boy said something I couldn't understand. I didn't see how this kid was ever going to have any friends. One thing about a friend: you need to be able to yell his name. But this name! I couldn't even tell how many letters there were among all the loops and lines. All I could tell was the "K" at the beginning and the "e" at the end.

So I went to work with those.

Usually apostrophes are stupid. You take out one letter and you put in one apostrophe—"wouldn't," "aren't," "it's," "we're"—so you don't save any time or energy or pencil lead; you've just got another stupid rule to remember.

But I made this apostrophe really do a job! I wrote the "K" and the "e" of the boy's name and jabbed in an apostrophe instead of the whole mess in the middle. I squeezed his whole long name down to "K'e."

"Key," I said. It could be written in a second and yelled in a second—a very good name for a friend.

"K'e," I wrote at the top of the boy's paper. I pointed to the boy and said, "K'e." The boy nodded.

"K'e," said K'e. He said it.

So that's how his name got changed, by just me and an apostrophe.

I decided I would help K'e with something else. I wrote "Mrs. White's class" and "September 28" under my name on my own paper. I showed K'e how to write this official information on his paper. I wrote "Language Arts" in the middle of the top of my page. K'e did the same. When I knew what K'e was writing, I could read his beautiful handwriting perfectly.

When Mrs. White asked for our papers, she would see that K'e had learned all that. I felt so good I tried to be interested in what she was teaching. She was discussing fantasy descriptions, trying to get us to imagine underwater scenes.

"Pretend you are a shark," she said. "A great ugly beast, hated by all the other creatures of the sea. You swim along, in the cold, gray sea. It's easy to be afraid of sharks and to hate them. But how would it feel to *be* a shark? I want each of you to pretend you are a shark and to write an imaginary description of a shark's world."

How could Mrs. White take something as interesting as sharks and make them so boring? Be a shark? Nobody wanted to *be* a shark. The whole point of sharks was the danger. Phillip and I rolled our eyes at each other at such a stupid assignment.

Then I looked at K'e's paper. If there was one word in the whole English language that boy understood, it was "shark."

A great white shark crashed through churning water across K'e's paper, right under "Language Arts." Its dorsal fin curved like an executioner's knife. Its eye was mean, and its pointed teeth were threatening. Best of all, the shark was racing, with open jaws, right toward—tah,tah, ladies and gentlemen—Sam Diefenbach! It said so, right on the drawing. K'e had copied my name from my paper. He had put a neat little arrow from the name to the brave diver who awaited the charging monster with his knife in his left hand and his spear in his right. *That*, Mrs. White, is what a shark is all about.

K'e drew scenes right out of my imagination, except he made my hair hang down in my face too much. He held the drawing out to me.

"Thank you," I said, and pushed the hair up out of my face.

"Yeah," K'e said. It was the first thing I had ever

heard him say, besides his confusing long name and his good new short one.

He pointed to my name, then to me.

"Yeah," I said.

He shook his head. He pointed to my name, and moved his mouth around as if he had something stuck in his teeth.

"Sam," I said.

"Sam," K'e said. He spoke the way he wrote, very clearly, but you wouldn't understand what he said unless you already knew what he was saying. "Sam," he said. "Yeah."

He stuck out his hand. I looked around to make sure the other kids weren't looking. In my country mostly men shook hands, not kids. I did it real fast, but it was okay. It felt good.

Before the end of class I wrote a brief description of sharks. I also got K'e to write his name and the other information on one more piece of paper, and then I took that one away from him fast, before he could start drawing on it. I showed it to Mrs. White, and she was very pleased with how much I had been able to teach the new boy. Of course, there were some things Mrs. White didn't know.

I placed the drawing of Sam Diefenbach and the shark between pages of my notebook so it wouldn't get torn. When I got home, I taped it on the wall above my bed, near my mom's alligator picture.

I picked up the co-op without talking to anyone there and ate grapes all the way home. Then I ate both halves of a big pink grapefruit while I watched my dad cook. Susan and Whit were late. "Those two are always late," Dad said. The only good thing about them.

Dad shaved a tiny strip of plastic off each side of the fuselage, and then my model fit perfectly. I worked on it most of the evening. I came out only to eat my grilled cheese when they had dinner.

"Fabulous eggplant, Robbie," Susan said. "How did you do it?"

Oh, brother.

"It's great," Whit said. "Why don't you try some, Sam?"

"It's from the co-op," was all I said. I held my grilled cheese high, and with my tongue collected all the cheese strings from my last bite.

For the salad Dad had chopped up cucumbers and white radishes and mixed them up in yogurt. White plus white in white equals boring white. A typical co-op supper.

"Fabulous salad, Robbie," Whit said.

I knew those two were fakers, exaggerating about eggplants and yukky white salads. Well, if that was the kind of friends he wanted, okay. I had a friend who could exaggerate about great white sharks—and me.

4
That Park of Crazies

One Saturday I came in after breakfast to watch
Robbie shaving neatly and carefully around his beard,
before he went to the office to work on another of
his housing reports. My dad thinks about low-income
housing, then he writes about it; that's his job. He
put dabs of shaving cream on my cheeks and on my
nose.

"Hey, Dad! I'm too old for that," I said. "I wish it
were whipped cream."

"If it were whipped cream, I'd be shaving all day
long." He mushed his cheeks around to be sure he
was getting all the hairs off. "Hey, Sam. I'm sorry

about having to work again. You're a real trooper about it."

"I ain't no trooper. I think it stinks. Dad, do you get paid more when you work on Saturday?"

"No." I didn't think so. "It would be nice if I did, but it's all part of the job. And I like this work, Sam. I just don't like to work Saturdays and miss being with you."

Then why do it? This guy is worried about money, but he's working for free on Saturdays when we could be biking or going to the pet store. We used to go to the pet store almost every weekend to see the puppies.

He finished shaving and left, and that left me to go meet Phillip, to track the drunken bum. His mother had told him it was a nice fall day, and he should get some nice fresh air. She always had some reason for him to get some nice fresh air. Tracking the bum was probably not one of her reasons, but that's what we were going to do. It was one of Phillip's favorite games.

Actually, there wasn't much to the game of tracking the bum. We would follow him, waiting, watching, hoping, and afraid that something terrible would happen. It never did.

"The little park, first," Phillip said as we started. "That's the place all the crazies hang out."

"I wonder where he lives," I said.

"Probably sleeps on the benches, covered with a newspaper," Phillip said.

I saw the drunken bum often, walking quickly along the streets, or in the little park on Q Street, where he often slept, or picking through the trash cans in the big park in Dupont Circle to get what was left of people's lunches. You could recognize him a block away by the clothes he wore—a filthy fancy coat with the pockets torn and hanging, and high, worn-out boots.

Phillip and I sighted him a few blocks up the avenue, and we raced past the shops and restaurants and around and between the slow walkers. Those new sneakers were dirty now, really mine; I loved making the fast stops and the fast starts. I knew I could tear out of there if the bum even looked at me. We ran to within twenty feet of him, our usual tracking distance.

The bum stopped at a curb by the wide avenue, swaying.

"Wait for the light, wait for the light," I said it like a prayer.

"Actually, he probably tells the traffic by the vibrations, the way a snake does," Phillip said.

"I hope he doesn't get hit."

"If he does," Phillip said, "I hope I see it. There's supposed to be so many traffic accidents, but I never get to see any of them."

The bum lunged into the traffic with his nervous swaying walk, barely missing the cars. The light changed, and we raced across, a block below him. He was coming fast.

"Stand back and let him pass!" Phillip said. "Don't let him breathe on you. The alcohol could knock you out!"

I pressed my back against a store window. I hated being close to the bum. He let nothing stand in his way. Once I saw him slam right between two men who were talking to each other, just slam right through.

He walked fast, on the tips of his toes, talking angrily to himself. The bum walked inside that murmur of his own conversations the way he walked inside his haze of alcohol, inside the long dirty coat he never took off.

We could feel his anger inside, burning low, ready to explode out through him, flaming mad. That's what we were waiting to see. That's why, every time, we dared ourselves to get closer.

Phillip ran ahead. Phillip doesn't run very well. He's a little fat, and he wears his jeans too tight. I watched him for a minute, but he didn't get really close. Phillip was scared, too.

Then I saw K'e. He was far down a side street, turning circles on his bicycle in the middle of the street. He waved, and I waved back.

K'e was one of my best friends in school now. He

had given me some exciting pictures. But out of school we never got together. Once I asked him for his phone number, but he didn't seem to understand. Maybe he didn't have a phone. After school he always disappeared. I saw him on his bike, here and there, never in one particular place or going in one particular direction. Usually he was doing some dangerous trick in the middle of the street. My dad wouldn't even let me ride in the street.

Now he turned, riding no-hands, down the wrong side of the street. When I glanced away, to find Phillip, and then looked back, K'e was gone, and then I almost bumped into Phillip, who was yelling, "He's going to the little park!" So I went on with Phillip.

By the time we got there, the bum was down on his belly, reaching under one of the benches, into a small bush.

"He's after a bottle," Phillip said. "Let's sit down here."

We sat on a bench near a woman who seemed okay; she wasn't too old, and she was eating doughnuts. But her hair was shaggy and her glasses hung on the end of her nose. We didn't sit too close.

Phillip said, "That dumb bum. You wait for him to do something dangerous, and all he does is lie under a bench. If he doesn't do something good pretty soon, I'm not going to play this game any more."

"Him dangerous?" the woman with the doughnuts said. "Hah! He's just a smelly old rag."

Phillip didn't answer her. "Hey, Sam!" he said after a minute. "Have you ever touched the third rail?" He waved his arm in the direction of the Metro station entrance and grinned a big grin. "Let's go down and you touch the third rail."

"That rail carries seven hundred and fifty volts," I said.

"It's an experiment, Sam." Phillip watched me out of the sides of his eyes. In a second he grinned again. "Kill you for sure."

The woman gave a loud laugh. "Hah! That would really zap you out to the airport!"

This time Phillip laughed with her.

"Hey, kid. You want a doughnut?" She held out her bag to him.

"Sure!" Phillip said.

"You?" She held the bag for me.

"No, thanks," I said.

The woman took another herself. "I come over here to buy them. There's a store sells day-old real cheap."

"Why don't you take one, Sam?" Phillip said it so loud I was embarrassed.

"I'm not supposed to take food from strangers," I whispered. A thousand times, a thousand times, Robbie tells me.

"Sam?" Phillip said, still loud. "She's eating them herself. What do you think, she's feeding herself some poison?"

"Hah!" The woman held out the bag. Phillip took another, but I shook my head.

"Sam, you can't always do what your father says, your whole life!" Phillip said. His doughnut looked delicious.

"His father's damn right!" the woman said, giving me a friendly nod. "You should never take food from a stranger. There's all kinds of nuts in this world."

"I'll say," Phillip muttered.

"I just forgot I was a stranger. Hah!"

I kind of liked that woman. Still, I didn't take one of her doughnuts.

The drunken bum gave a snort and came out from under the bench. Phillip and I sat up and waited, ready to run if we had to. But all he did was climb onto the bench and lie down with his eyes closed.

Phillip walked over, carefully at first, then very close. He touched a loose flap at the bottom of the bum's coat, then pulled his finger away as if it had been burnt. But he gave me a triumphant smile. That's what he had always wanted to do—touch the bum.

"I guess that's his home bench," he said, settling down again between me and the woman, and stretching out his legs.

"Some home sweet home," said the woman.

"I wouldn't like to be a bum," I said. "I wouldn't want to be poor like that."

"I could never be that kind of person," Phillip said. "I could never be such a drunken, poor, smelly person." He stared at the bum for a moment. "That boring bum. He never does anything crazy. It's disgusting." He waited a minute to see if anything would happen. "Hey, Sam! I'm going to go as a drunken bum on Halloween. Dress up in raggedy clothes. I can be a better bum than that old guy." He stood up. "I'm supposed to be home now," he said. "See ya, Sam." And he was gone.

The bum hadn't moved at all. I couldn't see him breathe, even. The woman was trying to get a dog to eat a chocolate doughnut—a ratty dog, a drunken bum of a dog, and she was trying to feed him a chocolate doughnut! I didn't want to be left alone with her. I got up and walked over to the park entrance, ready to move out of there fast.

I have to be able to move fast in the city streets and to think fast, to take care of myself. So I have my ways. I can walk like I know what I want and where I want to go. I can say "no" strongly and politely, without showing I'm afraid. And if I have to, I can run like crazy. But I didn't want to leave now. That poor old bum might be dying.

I watched Phillip tear off across the avenue. I hated the way he was about the bum. I wasn't sure I would play again with him, either, maybe.

Suddenly the bum drew a loud snorting breath and heaved himself up. His eyes were pointed in my direction, but I couldn't tell whether they could see anything, they were so red and wet. His body was leaning toward me, but his feet didn't move.

He began talking and looking at the woman, as if he were talking about her. She was breaking off doughnut pieces for that grungy dog and paying no attention. The man's voice got louder and angrier, but I couldn't understand the words.

He started going through his pockets. I should have left then. But I wanted to know what he was looking for.

He couldn't find it. He mumbled into the collar of his coat as his hands went here and there over his body and his clothes, searching the same places over and over. At last he took out a piece of paper money. It was brand-new, but it looked funny, not like a dollar. I thought it might be a twenty, but I couldn't believe that. Anyway, a dollar or twenty dollars, where would a bum get brand-new money?

He began talking loudly again, and looking at me as if I should be paying attention. He walked straight over to me, straight and strong, not at all as if he were about to fall. He held the money out to me. It was a twenty.

I shook my head.

His voice got louder and angrier. He said something about the dog. He wanted me to buy the dog some meat. The dog shouldn't be eating doughnuts, he said. He wanted me to take the money and go to the store and buy the dog some good meat.

"Hah!" said the woman. "I'll take it."

The bum was standing right over me, swaying again, stinking and smelling and holding out the money. I stepped back.

"No, thank you," I said.

With a swear word at me, and a swear word at her, and an angry swing of his arm, he turned and sat down right there on the bench. He was talking at the money now, telling his plans. He was flinging and folding his arms, shouting, and doing nothing.

The woman was calling, too, holding out another chocolate doughnut toward the dog. The dog walked slowly across the park and sat scratching his fleas, scratching and looking around and scratching again.

So that's when I left, left the two of them, one talking to the money, one talking to the dog. I left that park of crazies.

About a block from the park, when I couldn't see or hear them any longer, I started to run. There was no danger. I just needed to run.

5
POW!

After I ran about three blocks, I slowed to a walk. I turned into our block—nothing else to do. But I didn't want to go home. Dad wouldn't be there yet.

I heard sudden loud noises behind me, like a car out of control. Quickly I moved closer to the houses before I turned to look. It was K'e, on his bicycle, in the street. He was coming fast, making noises with his mouth, his head down, watching his feet pedaling, not watching at all where he was going. He was looking down so he didn't see me wave.

He put on speed until he reached the end of the block, and then, just before he slammed into the heavy traffic on 17th Street, he braked and turned and raised both arms, like a circus performer asking for applause. Asking me! He had known all the time I was there! He gave a yell and pedaled back, the wrong way down the center of our one-way street.

The only crash was a sound like screeching brakes and a loud pop, both of which came from K'e's mouth, not his bike. He pulled up on the sidewalk directly in front of me. "Hi," he said. He pointed to my building and to me. I wondered how he knew. K'e parked his bike by the steps and started up. I had a guest.

When we got upstairs, K'e took the key string from my neck. He unlocked the door, then stepped back and bowed to let me in first. That guy!

Inside, he took off his jacket, but not his cap. He loves that cap. It's a leather cap with a fleece lining and big ear flaps and a strap. It looks like an old-fashioned aviator's cap. K'e even wears it in school, as long as Mrs. White lets him get away with it. He looks like he's always ready for takeoff.

He walked around our apartment, touching every-thing he looked at, as if he had two kinds of eyes—in his head and in his fingers. I was a little worried. I wasn't supposed to have another kid in when I was alone.

"I'd better check with my dad," I told him.

He nodded. I didn't know whether he understood or not. K'e could understand a lot of English some-times. Sometimes not. He understood Mrs. White pretty well, but he could hardly understand anything the science teacher said. He never did the work she gave us. And he couldn't understand the boring art teacher, who had exactly the same projects over and over, every year for every class. K'e drew the whole time in art class; he never did any art.

When I called Dad, he didn't like the idea that K'e was there.

"Dad, he's very quiet. Please? We'll be quiet. We won't even talk."

"Well, it's all right to talk, Sam." Dad laughed. "What do you think? Can you handle it?"

"I think it's okay, Dad."

"Well, try it. Call me if you need me, and don't do anything rowdy. No experiments!"

"No experiments," I promised. "K'e draws the adventures—he doesn't do them himself." I didn't mention his bicycle riding.

"There's some tuna fish there for lunch, and put some lettuce on it, will you, for your vitamins? And make sure he calls his parents, to let them know where he is. I should be finished here in a few hours."

"I don't know if I can get him to call, Dad." I was sure I couldn't get K'e to call.

"Sam. Of course he must call. Right away. His mother may be worried."

"I don't even know if he's got a mother," I mumbled.

"Sam! Of course he has a mother. See you soon."

I don't. Have a mother. You dumb guy. I hung up.

I wasn't even sure K'e had a home. He seemed to live on his bicycle, moving all the time, somewhere, anywhere, on the streets of Washington, D.C.

I found him in the dining room. "You'd better call home," I said. I took him into the kitchen and held out the phone. "Call," I said. "Call your mother."

K'e made a face and pushed the phone away. "I don't call," he said. He opened the refrigerator.

I didn't know what to do. "Do you want something to eat?"

"Yeah," K'e said.

"Tuna fish?"

K'e shook his head. He looked at everything in the refrigerator; it took a long time.

I hoped K'e wouldn't ask for scrambled eggs. I knew how to cook scrambled eggs, excellently, with Cheddar cheese, but I wasn't supposed to use the stove when Dad was away. Probably cooking scrambled eggs was rowdy.

I wasn't sure K'e could even understand the idea that something wasn't allowed. I began to think that in some quiet way K'e was like Phillip, that anything could happen with him, just more quietly.

Finally K'e slammed the refrigerator door and said, "Yeah."

I thought for a minute. "Tuna fish?"

"Yeah."

I started making the sandwiches, toasting the rye

bread, opening the can and dumping the tuna fish into a bowl, mixing in mayonnaise and a sprinkle of dill weed and exactly one tablespoon of pickle relish.

When I turned to get the lettuce, I found K'e drawing on the refrigerator door with the water-soluble crayon that hung there. We used the door for writing messages, making lists, and just for doodling.

K'e was doodling on the refrigerator as it had never been doodled on before. He was working on a drawing Dad had made, the face of a smiling woman. K'e had drawn a pair of glasses on her and colored in her face and put on a neck scarf and changed her hair and made her look quite like Mrs. White. And now Mrs. White was about to be swallowed by a great white shark, which was surging up the door, spraying drops of salt water from its wide-open, tooth-filled jaws. Poor Mrs. White hung there, smiling sweetly with the smile that Dad had drawn, not knowing K'e's shark was about to wham her.

I put the sandwiches right on the kitchen table. I hate to wash dishes. Too bad I had to use glasses for the juice.

K'e opened his sandwich and looked in. He took out the lettuce and smelled the tuna.

"Fish?" he asked.

"Tuna fish," I said.

"Fish?" he asked, and pointed to the refrigerator shark.

"No."

47

K'e shrugged. He put the top back on his sandwich, but not the lettuce, and put the sandwich in
his mouth. He held it there for a moment, not taking
a bite, just breathing in the taste. Then he took it
out of his mouth again and took a long drink of juice.
When he finally started to eat, he chewed very fast,
like some kind of eating machine.

"Do you like it?" I asked.

"Nah," K'e said. He smiled and said, "I don't eat
fish," but he kept on eating. He was very confusing,
what he said and what he did.

There wasn't much to talk about with someone
who doesn't talk. While I was wondering what to do
next, K'e started drawing on the kitchen table. I guess
he thought since we wrote on the refrigerator, it was
okay to write on all our furniture.

"Oh! No!" I said. "K'e? Don't draw on the table.
Wait, I'll get you some paper." I brought him a pencil
and some plain paper. Then he finished his sandwich
and juice, using his left hand, and drew with his
right.

He drew a submarine. When he was done with the
outline, he looked up to see how I liked it.

"Good," I said. "Submarine," I said, in case he
didn't know the word.

"Submarine," he said, and went back to work. He
drew a periscope and looked at me.

"Periscope," I said.

He nodded. "Radar periscope," he said. I didn't

48

know there was such a thing. Maybe there wasn't.

K'e drew several parts I couldn't identify, so I brought in the World Book, Volume "So-Sz." There were four pages on submarines, old ones and modern. K'e got very excited, leafing back and forth, copying out parts. He ended up with a supercolossal submarine, completely covered with all kinds of old and new equipment, commanded by two captains, K'e and me, one standing at each end, peering through our telescopes.

"That's good," I said. I pushed my hair back from my face.

K'e immediately began another picture. As soon as I saw he was making a helicopter, I brought in Volume "H."

When I left a little later to get Volume "Sa-Sn," for sharks, K'e followed to see where all these wonderful books came from. He ran his finger down the whole row and looked in several. He found a good section on Jet Propulsion and took that book into the kitchen.

By the time Dad came home, most of the encyclopedia was in the kitchen, and we had pictures of me and K'e as captains, divers, drivers, pilots, and fighters, always being brave. K'e was working on a jungle scene, a tiger and a man fighting. I didn't know yet if it was him or me.

"Do you have real jungles and tigers near your home, K'e?" I asked.

He shook his head fast, as if he didn't even want to talk about it. A moment later he said, "I don't go by jungle."

That's when Robbie came in. As I introduced them, I remembered that I had not tried again to get K'e to call home. I waited for Dad to ask and get mad. He did. Right away, he began a speech saying I could not have visitors unless I took full responsibility and insisted they obey the family rules. Oh, brother.

K'e took care of me. He tapped Robbie gently and showed him the new drawing, a tiger with enormous eyes and teeth, standing high on his hind legs in the midst of a thick tropical jungle. The tiger was being held off by—tah, tah, ladies and gentlemen, you guessed it—Robbie Diefenbach! Absolutely, it was him: the neat curly beard, the cool dark glasses, the same jeans and sneakers he was wearing at that very moment. Bare to the waist, with a chest like Superman's, he was about to plunge his curved hunting knife into the leaping tiger's heart.

Dad stopped talking, but his mouth stayed open. He probably hadn't imagined himself like that since he was a sixth grader.

"Me?" he asked.

"Yeah," K'e said, nodding seriously, pointing from the drawing to the man. And he made one of those neat little arrows and wrote in his very neat script, "Mrs. Diefenbach." Dad was so pleased, smiling and blushing, he didn't even fix the "Mrs." yet.

50

"Me?" He shook his head, with a huge smile. "It does look a little like me."

K'e smiled and shrugged. He dropped his pencil and moved suddenly to a crouching position. He moved across the floor hunching his shoulders, rocking back and forth, his cap strap swinging under his chin, and coming up with a huge punching motion toward Dad. His fist landed heavily in the air. "Pow!" he said.

Dad jumped back. But K'e grinned and pointed to him. Dad understood then and imitated K'e. Sock, sock; pow, pow; boxing in the air. He nodded at K'e, meaning, Am I doing it right?

K'e nodded and made the pow motion again. Dad followed, the two of them backing and circling around the dining room, around the living room, Dad following K'e's backward lead, punching in the air, rocking up and down.

"Okay," said K'e.

"Yeah!" K'e said.

" 'Bye," K'e said, and grabbed his jacket and slipped backward, still crouching, out the front door, going back, I guess, to the parents, I guess, with whom, I guess, he lived. I heard him racing down the stairs.

I shut the door, and we were alone. I didn't know whether to laugh or worry.

"Yeah?" Dad asked me. "What did he mean, 'Yeah'?"

"Yeah, that picture is you."

"Oh." Dad went to look at the picture again. "Pow!" I heard him say. I waited for him to get mad again about K'e's not calling home, but he seemed to have forgotten. K'e had completely bamboozled him. Robbie erased the "s" from "Mrs. Diefenbach" and put the tiger-killing picture in his briefcase. "Won't that look great on my bulletin board?"

"Yeah," I said. "Yeah!" K'e didn't talk much, but he sure got Robbie to shut up for once about all that. K'e sure took care of me.

Pow! was right.

6
Kristie Comes, and Goes

One day, early in December, when it was getting dark earlier and windy cold and I couldn't play outside long after school, I came home to find the living room a familiar total mess.

Robbie had put newspapers all over the rug. Wooden crates and cardboard boxes of vegetables and fruits from the wholesale markets were lined up across one end of the room. Under the corners of the boxes, the newspapers showed damp splotches of gray. I kicked a box of cabbages. Cabbage! I went into the kitchen. The only good thing about our turn to distribute the co-op food was that Dad would be home early.

I made myself a snack and watched reruns on television until almost time for him to come. I lined up twelve brown grocery bags on the living room floor. Then I made myself a grilled cheese and a blended OJ on ice. I knew I wasn't going to like supper. I sat on my haunches, eating and looking at the crates and bags, hating the co-op.

"Hi, Sam," Dad said, coming in the door. "What's good?"

"Pineapples and grapefruit." The only good things in this co-op came from Florida. "I ain't eatin' any cabbage."

"I thought the only thing you ain't eatin' is eggplant." Dad laughed. "Come on, Sam."

"Can I have the pineapple tonight, Dad? The way I like it with honey and lemon juice? I'll make it."

"Tonight! Good news tonight, Sam. Kristie's coming over."

"Kristie? Kristie! Kristie!"

Kristie is my mom's sister. She's a lawyer and she goes all over the country, where she has her testimonies and her hearings. Even when she's home, she has to work hard, so she can't come over much. That's why she sends me postcards from all her trips. With my mom away in Florida, and my grandparents in Pittsburgh, Kristie was the only person in our family we saw very much.

Kristie smells good. I pass a lot of people on their

way to work when I'm walking to school, and I smell
their morning smells—perfume and shaving lotion.
The way those people smell in the morning is the
way Kristie smells all the time. I love it when she
comes.

"She saw Sheila a few days ago, Sam, and she's
got lots of news and love for you. Let's get this co-
op work out of the way and make her a super
supper."

While I opened the crates and boxes, Dad checked
the co-op record book and did the math. Divide 48
grapefruit by 12, divide 18 pineapples by 12, divide
50 pounds of onions by 12.

I cut open the huge sack of onions with my pock-
etknife and began my trips back and forth across the
living room, taking ten onions to each brown bag.
That got me only two-thirds down the sack, so I made
a second distribution of five onions each, then a third
trip with one more for almost everyone.

I was putting seven bananas in each bag, and Robbie was cutting a few pineapples and cabbages in
half, when the doorbell rang.

"Kristie!" I yelled, and Kristie it was, looking wonderful as usual in a blue suit and one of those pink
ladies' blouses and her long black hair braided and
coiled up around her head. She always carried a
small red pocketbook over her shoulder and a small
red briefcase in her hand. And almost always she

wore red shoes. She has four pairs. Once, when I was little, I asked her why she had so many red ones. She said, "Didn't you see *The Wizard of Oz*? I'm the Wicked Witch of the West. My red shoes take me wherever I want to go." Kristie is *not* the Wicked Witch of the West, but I remembered her joke because she goes around so much.

She gave me a long tight hug. Her jacket was warm, and her cheek was cool and smooth. She gave Dad a big hug, too. "Woooo! It's good to be here! Too many hotels last month, Rob. How are you?"

She took off her jacket and let her long braid down and kicked her red shoes under the couch. "Off with the disguise!" When she looked around the room, she burst out laughing. "I know I like my fruit and veggies, Rob, but you didn't have to get this much! Have you left the housing business and gone into groceries? May I?" She held up a cucumber.

"Sure. Take them all," I said.

Kristie sliced the skin off, and cut herself a big chunk. "Oh, that's good. Robbie, what is all this?"

Dad gave her his speech about the co-op. And he told her how cheap all that stuff was, so he *was* worried about money. I knew that was why.

While he was talking, Kristie helped us finish the distribution. Then we took our own bag into the kitchen and unpacked it all again and started making supper. I cut the pineapple into bite-size triangles, then stirred in the honey and lemon juice. The best. I took a few tastes and gave Kristie a few tastes and Dad a few tastes, and there was still plenty left for supper.

Dad cooked the cabbage with onions and hamburger and put yogurt on top. Kristie made a cucumber salad, and I made myself another grilled cheese. All this time, the co-op people were interrupting our talk, coming to get their food.

"I saw your momma, kiddo. I had to be in Miami, and I went out and spent the whole weekend with her. She sent you a thousand hugs and fourteen kisses." Kristie kissed me and kissed me all over my head, and I liked it a lot, even if I was too old for that.

"And she sent you a present, which I have safely here in my bulging briefcase, I hope." She began looking for it among all her papers and her pads. "Sheila is fantastic, Rob. The clinic is going great. She's fighting the bureaucrats up and down the streets, driving them crazy. I worked with her all Saturday, straightening out some of the paperwork. I had a ball. Sheila looks good. She works too hard, that's all."

My mom worked Saturdays, too. Maybe she at least got paid for it. I interrupted Kristie. "Is Sheila rich?"

"No," Dad said, fast.

Kristie grinned at him and shook her head at me

and went on with her story. I was still waiting for my present. "So I rented a car on Sunday, and whisked her out of town. When she realized there was no hope of getting back in time to do anything, she relaxed and we had a great time. Here it is, kiddo." Kristie handed me the package and walked over to the stove and took a taste from the pan. "Fabulous cabbage," she said.

I held the present for a moment, just looking at it. My own mother had folded that wrapping and put on that tape and sent that present to me.

I didn't know Sheila well any more. I was confused about why my parents didn't stay together. My father and I had talked about it, two times, but I was still confused. My mother was a kind of friend I had, far away, who sent me presents, sometimes, and called me, sometimes, and wrote to me, sometimes. I hadn't seen her for two years. I didn't even know if I missed her any more.

Slowly I opened Sheila's present. It was perfect. I didn't know what it was, but it was beautiful. It was glass, a triangle of glass about seven inches long. It was shiny, but soft and frosty on one side. I looked through it, and it moved things around. I ran my finger over the glass, the smooth part and the frosty part. I put the glass back in its little soft case and put it in my pocket. It was a perfect present.

"Try it in the sunlight tomorrow, Sam," Kristie

said. She was eating yogurt from the carton and watching me, smiling as if something sad had happened. I didn't see how someone who smelled so sweet could like yogurt. "It's a prism," she said.

I wished Kristie would tell more about Sheila's health clinic, and Sheila, but I felt shy asking about my mom. I didn't know what I wanted to know, exactly, or even what I was supposed to know, about my mother, who was gone. I just wanted them to talk about her.

Instead, while we set the table and started to eat, Kristie told about her trips and the things she did, and Dad kept bugging her about how she traveled too much. She always took the trips, and he always bugged her. "You wear yourself out," he said. "You give up too much."

"There are some great things about traveling, Rob. I know most of the big cities, I see so many things. But, like it or not, I have to travel. This lawyering is very competitive. If I won't travel, they'll find someone who will. The funny thing is, I used to love it. When I was in college and in law school, I used to go whenever I got the chance. I'd just take off. It was the only thing to do when I got the crazies."

The crazies! Phillip calls those bums the crazies, but Kristie gets the crazies herself! Two kinds: the people crazies, and the crazies inside. I think I get the inside crazies sometimes.

"My sophomore year in college," she was saying, "I didn't have a summer job, and I went all over the West, traveling on my thumb."

Quickly I swallowed my mouthful of grilled cheese. "Huh? How did you go?"

"Hitchhiking, Sam," Kristie said. "You stand by a road that goes where you want to go, and you hold out your thumb. Someone stops, you climb in, and you're off on a free ride. It's great." She stuck out her thumb and jerked her arm in a cocky way.

I tried it. It felt good.

"And it's incredibly dangerous, Sam." Dad didn't like her to say that stuff in front of me, I could tell. "You don't know who's going to pick you up, or why, or where they're going to take you."

"Hey! I've never had any trouble. I haven't done it much since then, but once last year we had terrific pressure on a case—we'd been working weekends and nights for three straight weeks, and they finally gave me a week off. I had the crazies, bad. I had to go somewhere else! Not get there so much as just go! I stuck out the old thumb, and it was great. You meet good people, traveling that way. People are nice." She smiled at me.

"I like to feel everyone is my friend, too," Dad said. "But you have to be careful. There are crazy people in the world. Just because you never had trouble doesn't mean it would be safe next time."

"Oh, Rob, you can run into trouble walking around

the corner to buy cigarettes." Kristie smokes, too. "I can handle a situation."

"People think they can. Sometimes they can't."

"Okay, Rob, okay! Hey, Sam, have you been to the Air and Space lately?"

Kristie took me to the Air and Space Museum last year. It's the best.

"No. You want to go this weekend?"

"I'm sorry, kiddo. I'd love to, but I'm going to New Orleans on Sunday, and I have to spend Saturday preparing my stuff. Maybe we could go after January fifteenth. The pressure should ease up a little then."

"Okay," I said. I think Kristie works even more than Robbie.

After dinner I lay on the living room couch between my dad and Kristie, like a little kid again, listening to them talk, getting sleepy, watching the last people come for their vegetable bags.

Kristie and Dad were still talking, talking about the government now. A thousand times they said the same old things. She had to keep telling him about some man she thought was an idiot. I like it when they talk about the government because they don't agree about that either, and sometimes I can tell from their voices that Kristie is right. But even if they talked too much, I didn't care; when Kristie was there, our family seemed much bigger, much nicer. I pressed my nose against her sleeve, to smell the good smell.

I thought about traveling myself. Maybe I needed to travel, like Kristie did. It sounded great: get the crazies and go! Maybe going by thumb was a way I could travel by myself, to West Virginia, maybe, to that good camp; to Pittsburgh, to see my grandparents; to Florida.

And so what, maybe, if Robbie Diefenbach didn't like the idea? Someday, I thought. Someday I'm going to leave this place, leave and go and see some things.

Maybe it was time to see if I could do something my father didn't like. Phillip ate that woman's doughnuts, and he didn't die. And K'e didn't call home, and he's okay. And Kristie travels by her thumb sometimes, and she has more fun than anyone else I know. And my father doesn't like any of that, and so what, maybe? I twisted the end of Kristie's long black braid around my finger. My hair is black like hers; Robbie's hair, and his beard, too, is dark red-brown. She winked a long private wink to me.

Robbie told Kristie about my school, about what a good reader I was, but how he was afraid I was getting behind in math, about how the science program was no good, about how proud he was that I was getting so independent. Kristie had answers for everything.

"Hey!" I made my voice sleepy, and I gave Dad a poke with my foot, and I smiled at Kristie, all at once. "Why are you talking so much about me?"

"Because we love you, kiddo," Kristie said. So then I did go to sleep.

I wasn't sure: maybe I heard and maybe I didn't hear Robbie tell Kristie about how expensive everything was getting, about how our rent was going up and the whole neighborhood was costing more to live in. I wished I knew if we were poor, and I wished Dad would talk to me about that. He had never told me how a kidnapper would know that your dad didn't have much money, and know not to take you.

When I woke up, Kristie was already gone. Dad helped me get to bed. I was so sleepy he had to remind me to wash my face and brush my teeth.

"Sam," he said. "Let's go to the Air and Space over your Christmas vacation. I could take a day off. . . ."

"Really, Dad? Could you really do that?" I can go down to the Mall by myself, on the Metro; it's just more fun with him.

"Sure. Congress won't be in session then, and there won't be much going on. And winter's a good time—there aren't so many tourists."

"Okay! I'd like that." I woke up a little more. "Dad?" It was hard to say it right. "The best part of Kristie coming is when she comes."

"What do you mean, Sam?"

"We get so happy when she comes, but then she gets more quiet and she talks to you so much. Kristie does the interesting things in this family, but when she talks it's not so interesting. And then she goes away, traveling again. Leaving."

"Is that the way it is, Sam?"

"Yes."

"Do you feel bad that you have to stay?"

"Yeah. I'd like to go! Fast wheels, faster than a bike." I made the thumb sign.

"You're a little young for that, son," Dad said softly. "You can get into big trouble with that. Sleep now."

After he left, I felt dreamy, sleepy. Trouble seemed far away.

7
Air and Space

Some years we go to Pittsburgh to visit my grand-parents over Christmas vacation, but this year we didn't; I don't really know why. But I had a good vacation, and Dad did take me to the Air and Space Museum. It was a warm and sunny day—I wore shorts in December!

I always loved that place. The Air and Space has the Wright Brothers' first airplane, and the Apollo spaceship that carried the first man to walk on the moon, and it has almost every kind of air- and space-ship in between.

My favorite is the Lockheed F-104A Starfighter,

the first fighter plane capable of Mach 2, twice the speed of sound. It's beautiful, blue and white and gold. It hangs in the air in a climbing position, as if all I would have to do is push a button and it would flash and thunder away. Even Robbie said it was beautiful.

I always look at the lunar rover, the kind of car the astronauts drove around the moon. The rover looks more like something a kid made with Tinkertoys or Lego pieces than a real car.

"That's the space ride for me!" Robbie said. "I'd love to bounce over the moon in that one, in almost no gravity. I'll leave the rockets to you, Sam, and I'll take that bouncing rover."

Downstairs, in the helicopter room, I told Dad, "K'e would like this place."

"Would you like to bring him here with us sometime?"

"I don't know," I said. "I don't even know if he's got a phone, remember?"

Dad laughed. "Are you about done?" he asked. "I'd like to walk over to the Freer Gallery and rest my eyes with those soft Oriental colors."

Outside, I led the way along the Mall, moving at a slight angle, across.

The Mall is the long, flat park that runs from the Washington Monument to Capitol Hill, with the Smithsonian museum buildings all along the sides. In the spring, when the grass is strong and green, people play softball and Frisbee in the middle, and the joggers jog around the edges. There are some driveways along the edges, too, for cars and for the tourist buses to park.

Only three things are allowed on the Mall: the merry-go-round by the Arts and Industries building, the big, plastic triceratops by the Natural History Museum for kids to climb on, and the red and glass and gold popcorn wagon, which is sometimes here and sometimes there, but I always find it. I don't know who decided those were the three things that could be allowed on the Mall, but he chose the right ones. And, of course, there are refreshment stands.

In winter it was not quite so good: the dinosaur was slippery if it was wet, and the merry-go-round was shut down. The grass had lots of bare, muddy places. The cold wet had come through the sneaker holes I had made dragging my toes, and reminded me it was December, even if the air was warm.

Dad didn't notice that I wasn't heading toward the Freer. Or maybe he did notice, and for once he didn't care. He didn't seem surprised when I stopped and we were standing in line at a refreshment stand.

He had coffee, and I had an ice cream stick. We sat on a dry patch of grass and watched the pigeons. I could see the American History Museum; if Kristie was free sometime, maybe we could go there, too. The red shoes from the Oz movie are in there. I bet Kristie didn't know that.

"Dad?" I said, but not until I was licking the last bit of ice cream off my stick. "I've been to the Freer a thousand times, and I've already been once this year. You go, okay? I've got some money, and I'll get popcorn and wait out here." Popcorn is the most nourishing snack food there is. That was sort of one of Robbie's rules, one of the good ones.

He laughed. "Okay, Sam. I won't stay long."

"Thank you!" I shouted. I hadn't expected it to work. Two snacks, even if I was paying for one of them! I leaped to my feet to make my getaway.

"Hang on, Sam," Dad said. "Here. Watch for me in about half an hour." He took out the fancy gold pocket watch that had belonged to his great-uncle. He wore it every day, on a gold chain, stuck into his pants pocket. The only time he didn't wear it was when he asked me to wait for him. Then he would kneel and fasten the gold chain to my belt loop and tuck the watch safely into my deepest pocket. The weight of the watch in my pocket was a promise that my father would always come back.

"Thank you!" I said again, and ran toward the popcorn wagon, with jumps and hops and cartwheels on the way. In line, I checked to be sure the watch was safe, and waved back to Dad.

With my popcorn bag, I squatted under a tree near the roadway so I could watch the machine popping corn, the people inside the wagon bagging it, the people buying, and the Mall birds—pigeons and sparrows mostly—gathered around to snatch the spilled pieces.

I'd love to move like a sparrow. Pigeons looked clumsy, like dizzy fat men, walking in circles. But the light little sparrows hardly walked at all; they used their wings to go even a few feet. They were smart and seemed to get what they wanted. If I could ever be any animal, I'd be a sparrow, and fly.

I was getting too far down the popcorn bag too fast, so I leaned back against the tree, just thinking. Flying! Nothing in that whole museum could do what that little sparrow could do; nothing in that whole museum was as good as that tiny sparrow, zipping about, perfect control, no crashes, no fueling, no breaking down. Perfect! I imagined a sparrow sneaking into the Air and Space one night and showing those planes how to really fly.

"Hi," a voice said. "Mind if I sit here, too?"

I focused my eyes. Some guy was standing there, standing with his back to the sun; all I could see was brightness behind and a shadow over his face.

"Sure," I said. "I mean, no, sit down, sure." Reluctantly I came up out of my daydream, back out onto the sunny afternoon on the Mall, wondering why the man asked me, as if there weren't plenty of room on the whole long Mall.

The man sat down and closed his eyes. He turned his face up to the sun. His blond mustache glowed slightly, little hot curls of golden wire.

I closed my own eyes, to go back to imagining that sparrow.

"It's a warm day," the man said. "For December. My name's Bob."

So? I said, inside. "Yeah," was all I said out loud, trying not to let a conversation get started. I wasn't going to tell him my name. It couldn't hurt to talk to a stranger outside the Smithsonian, but I didn't want to talk. I wanted to think about all the places a sparrow could get to in the Air and Space.

"It's a good day for climbing that dinosaur," said this Bob, pointing to the triceratops. "Why don't you climb the dinosaur? Your legs look nice and strong."

I pulled up my socks. "I've done that," I said.

"Why don't you climb it now?" the man said. "I'd like to see you climb."

"No, thank you," I said, moving my eyes away from his staring eyes. Thank you? When someone says something dumb to you, it's hard not to say something dumb back. "I mean, I don't want to right now. I'm tired." That wasn't true, but still, I kept feeling I should be polite. "Do you want some pop-corn?" I held out the bag. I couldn't believe how dumb this dumb guy was making me.

"Yes, thank you," Bob said, but he took just a little, as if he didn't want any, but he was trying to be polite, too. Never take food from a stranger, I thought, and smiled at the backwards joke. The man smiled back. Yuk. "Thank you," he said again.

I didn't like his quiet voice, and him sitting so close, as if the two of us had a private place together on the Mall, as if we had secrets. I didn't want this Bob acting like my friend. I looked over my shoulder, but my father wasn't there.

Now the man leaned back on his arms and closed his eyes and lifted his face to the sun. Maybe he didn't need to talk any more. Maybe being polite had taken care of my problem.

I watched for a moment to be sure he kept his eyes closed. Good. I put the empty popcorn bag upside-down over my sneaker to remind me to throw it away, and went back to being a sparrow.

If a sparrow got loose in the Air and Space, no guard could catch it. It could fly up to the nose cones of the tallest rockets and sing. It could fly onto the Kitty Hawk and the Spirit of St. Louis. It could go up to the beautiful Lockheed 104A Starfighter, my favorite. Half plane, half rocket ship, sleek as a dolphin cutting through the waves, soaring blue and white and gold, from earth to heaven, mounting through the clouds into the most glorious sky, and ...! Oh, I could dream about it, flying up on it, a sparrow on the Starfighter flying up into the stars. I put out my thumb like Kristie taught me. Could a sparrow hitch a ride on a Starfighter?

"Do you like to hitch-hike? Would you like to go for a ride?"

The voice that asked the questions was not in my

71

head. I blinked my eyes and saw that I was holding out my thumb. I saw that guy, Bob, staring at me, hard.

"Oh," I said. "Hi."

"Come on." He stood up. "My car's not far. We'll go for a drive. We'll get something nice to eat."

Oh, brother. He just saw me eating popcorn.

Bob put on a big smile. "Come on," he said. "I'm your friend."

I couldn't stand him looking at me, but I was afraid to look away. Perhaps the man couldn't stand it, either; he looked down at his own feet. He was smiling at his own feet! He was talking, too, talking about ice cream, talking softly, talking about taking a ride.

I stood up. The popcorn bag crunched under my foot, but I didn't take my eyes off Bob. "I'm not hungry," I said, but that wasn't enough to end this business. I needed something better to get me out of there. I jammed my hands into my pockets, making my arms stiff. My hand closed around my great-great-uncle's gold pocket watch, my father's watch.

Bob was looking straight into my face, again, with his soft smile and his hard, hard eyes. He had his hands in his pockets, too. I hated him.

Why did he even think I would get into a car with a stranger? That I would ever take food from a stranger? How dumb did Bob think I was?

"No, thank you," I said, very politely. I took out my watch and looked at the time. "It's time for me to go now. I have to meet my father at the Freer Gallery. My father needs me," I said.

Immediately I turned my back on Bob and started across the Mall. I didn't run, but I walked fast. After I had gone far enough, I looked back. He was gone. My heart and my lungs and my gut got loose again. I walked back to pick up the torn popcorn bag and threw it in the trash.

When I got to the Freer, my father was just coming out. We decided to walk all the way home and let the warm day last as long as possible.

I stayed close to him all the way home. I didn't tell him about that Bob. I hadn't done anything wrong; in fact, I had done just what Dad would have wanted me to do. Still I was ashamed that a stranger would ask me to come for a ride.

By the time we got home, I felt a little better. At least I never got in his car. Someone taking me away from Dad would be the worst thing in the world.

8
A Problem
Like That

"The great strength of democracy," Mrs. White said, "is that every citizen is responsible."

Oh, brother. I stuck my pencil into the side of my sneaker and popped loose another piece of rubber.

We had finished fantasy. She had started us on realism. But the "real" things Mrs. White talked about in Language Arts never had anything to do with *my* real life. Her realism was as boring as Dad's work at the Institute for a Humanist Housing Policy, as boring as the front page of the *Washington Post*.

"Today," Mrs. White said, "we will be looking around us, at our city and our country."

Phillip was already kicking my leg. I wished I could see what K'e was drawing.

"In January each year," Mrs. White said, "the President gives the Congress his State of the Union message. This Thursday evening the President will go to Capitol Hill to speak to the Congress. I hope all of you will be watching his address on television."

"On television? Thursday?" Phillip asked quickly. We were all paying attention now. "What time?"

"At nine o'clock," Mrs. White said. A groan came from all over the room. Cecily slammed her desk top. There were a lot of good shows on Thursday night.

I couldn't believe my bad luck with this State of the Union business. Last Sunday, just when we were going to the pet store, my dad's office called him to come quick and write something about the State of the Union and low-income housing. He spent the whole afternoon. Now Mrs. White was bugging me about it in school. And on Thursday the President was going to mess up the TV schedule with it.

"In the State of the Union address," Mrs. White said, "the President tells us how he thinks the country is doing, the good things and the problems, and what we should do to make the country better."

"I know one thing," LaTonya said. "Food costs too much."

Mrs. White snapped her chalk hurrying to get that idea on the board. "Exactly, LaTonya. Food prices are high. Can anyone think of something else the President might mention?"

"The budget?"

"The budget." Mrs. White wrote that on the board.

"National parks," Phillip said. "We went to Cape Cod National Seashore last summer. I got sunburned. It was terrific."

"What about national parks, Phillip?" Mrs. White asked.

"Well, we should have more of them, all over the place. We should have Cape Cod closer to Washington. The drive was boring."

"I doubt even the President can do that, Phillip." But she wrote "More national parks" on the board. "Anna Maria?"

"Health? More clinics? To help take better care of people?"

Yeah. My mom. My mom, and my dad, too. Helping people. I never thought of them together that way before.

"Housing," I said, for my dad, and because it was less boring to say something than to say nothing. "We need more low-income housing."

Some of the kids said foreign policy and cheaper bus rides and civil rights and peace, but nobody was very interested, and pretty soon there were no more hands. Mrs. White looked at the clock, and most of the class looked, too. We still had a whole hour before recess.

76

K'e was hunched up over his picture. His hair was hanging down, and his cap strap was hanging down, and everything was wiggling while he drew and erased and drew again. It must be a good one, I thought.

"Does anyone have anything to add?" Mrs. White asked.

After a moment Anna Maria said, "Poor people?"

"What do you mean, Anna Maria? What might the President say about poor people?"

"Poor people and how they live," Anna Maria said. "How to help them?"

"Always picking through the garbage," Cecily said loudly.

"There's a lady comes in our alley all the time," LaTonya said, "all the time digging in the garbage cans. She has these bags. She finds things to put in her bags."

"She the one with the long purple coat?" Claudio asked.

That class hummed then! Finally Mrs. White had found a realism that was real.

"Yeah! That purple coat lady!"

"We got her in our alley, too."

"No teeth!" Cecily yelled.

"She does, too."

"No, she doesn't."

"She does, she does," said Claudio. "She's got four teeth. Up top. I seen them."

"She's just one of the crazies," Phillip said.

Mrs. White was trying to organize the discussion. "What do you think she's looking for in the trash cans?"

All the kids were waving their hands.

"She's looking for food!"

"Some of those poor people have to look for their clothes. It's terrible!" Cecily slammed her desk top. Cecily was mad so often it was boring.

"Some of them sell that junk."

I didn't mention the Pickers. I wasn't sure about them. I had finally gotten close to them, once, and they smelled of liquor. They didn't stink of it, like the bum, but they smelled of it. Also, I wasn't sure they were poor. Even with the real crazies, it was hard to know. That crazy lady and the drunken bum, yelling in the little park; she had all those doughnuts, and he had a brand-new twenty-dollar bill.

"Better not get near the purple coat lady," Cecily called out, trying to get the class excited again. "If you get too close, she'll scream you out of her sight and never take a breath."

That's how I feel when I have the crazies, pure yelling mad.

"She uses bad words," Ralph said.

Phillip said a few, quietly. Everyone heard, of course.

Mrs. White flicked the lights for attention.

"She said it, Mrs. White, I didn't." Phillip acted so innocent.

"We don't use those words in the classroom, Phillip.

"Class? Let's get back to the State of the Union. How can our country take responsibility for those less fortunate than ourselves? What can we ask our President to do?"

"Give them a job?"

"Those poor people got to have food!"

"Give them a good meal every day!"

"Also, he should stop people tearing down the old houses around here," LaTonya said. "Give those houses to the poor people so they won't be in the alley all the time. I don't like them in my alley."

"That's low-income housing," I said. "My dad does that."

"Well, when is he going to start doing it around here?"

I didn't answer her. The truth was, I didn't understand my dad's job. He said he figured out how much low-income housing would be needed in the future. Once his name was in the *Washington Post*, but I couldn't see that that did any good. Whenever I went over to his office, all I could see that his dumb office did was write papers and mail them around. His office never made homes for people, when the drunken bum, or that purple coat lady, or the Pickers, maybe, needed a place that same night. Or us, maybe, if our rent got too high.

Mrs. White's voice had changed, so I tuned in. She

was explaining the Language Arts assignment.

"I want you each to think about what you would ask the President to mention in the State of the Union address. You'll each write a letter to the President. Perhaps you want to discuss one of the issues listed on the board. Do your very best work, because we will be mailing these letters to the White House."

Everyone stopped talking, then, getting out papers and pencils, getting ready to work. Funny, I was thinking, we were going to be writing about some of our neighbors, the alley people, to our other neighbor, the President, who lived in the big white house not very far away. He was a neighbor I never saw, except on television.

Discussion time was over, but when Wilda raised her hand, Mrs. White called on her. Wilda rarely spoke.

"Mrs. White, I gave that purple coat lady a glass of water one time," Wilda said.

Every kid stopped to listen. Wilda would never lie or exaggerate like Cecily or Phillip.

"Did she yell at you?"

Wilda shook her head.

"Did she give you the glass back?"

Wilda nodded.

"Did she say thank you?"

"She just gave it back. She called me Sugar. She said, 'Here, Sugar.' "

"Were you afraid?"

Wilda shook her head.

"That was very nice of you, Wilda," Mrs. White said. "Very nice to think of it."

"It was hot," Wilda said, and Wilda didn't say anything more in class for a week.

"That was very nice of Wilda," Mrs. White said. "But, class, Wilda may not be there the next time that woman needs help. What can be done? Start your letters now."

The class was quiet, and no one looked at the clock again for a long time.

At recess I saw some kids around K'e's desk, and I went over. He had made a drawing of Wilda giving water to the purple coat lady. It was a calm picture, not his usual. K'e signed his name, his long name, and then he stood up and handed the picture to Wilda and shook her hand. "Congratulations," he said. Wilda nodded, and K'e sat down.

That afternoon Mrs. White worked with each of us to correct our letters and to make sure our ideas were clear. Anna Maria got to write the address on the envelope: "The President of the United States, The White House, Washington, D.C., 20500."

"Anyone can write to the President," Mrs. White said, as she sealed the fat envelope closed. "Remember that. And every citizen is responsible."

When I got home, I found a note from Dad, saying he would have to work very late, saying that I should call him to talk about what I could make myself for supper.

He had never done that to me before, left me for the whole afternoon, plus suppertime, plus the whole evening, plus I had to cook the whole supper myself.

Could you write to the President about a problem like that?

9
Happy Like Kristie

One sunny Saturday morning late in February, Dad and I were eating our pancakes. Hoping as usual, I asked Dad, "Do you have to work today?"

"No. The report's all done. I don't have to show up there till Monday morning."

"Well, good," I said. "Because it doesn't do any good. I mean what good does it do to write about housing in the year 2000? Excuse me, Dad, but I don't even know what housing means, your kind, that doesn't even build houses for people."

"If people read my reports, Sam, people who have something to say about housing policies, then my reports may do some good."

"Do you know where the Pickers live?"

"Who?"

"Never mind." Maybe the Pickers had no house at all. Maybe they just turned their cart upside down and crawled under.

"I know you don't like it when I have to work on weekends, Sam, but that's part of my job. And among other things, my job pays for those pancakes you love so dearly." Dad smiled.

Then he flipped over a page on his brain pad and unhitched his watch, and I remembered. He did have to go out, to a meeting of the co-op.

I could hardly believe so much fuss about a little food. When Robbie finally got bothered, when they gave us eggplant three weeks in a row, he just called everyone and organized a meeting.

"Why does it have to be on Saturday, Dad?"

"It was dumb, Sam. I'm sorry. It seemed the only time most people were free."

"You ain't free on Saturdays. Saturdays you got me."

"Yes. But . . ." Dad's voice was getting gruff. "You do dumb things, too, Sam."

"Hardly ever," I said. I was angry, too. It felt good letting my crazies come out, even if it was scary yelling back at my own father. "I'm tired of this Saturday business. You worry about being poor and you go away and work extra and you don't even get paid for it—"

"Sam. We are not poor. I don't get a huge salary, but we are very well off compared to most people. And part of my satisfaction in my job is helping some of those disadvantaged people. That's worth working some extra hours."

"Well, if we're not poor, why do we have to be in the stupid co-op just to get some stupid cheap vegetables? And you have to go to a stupid meeting the first Saturday you're free in a thousand years—"

"That's enough, Sam. I made a mistake about the meeting this morning, but Saturday work is part of my job, and we both, you and I, need me to keep this job. There are a thousand people in this city who can write reports, who would love my job. So think about that, will you, and lay off the carping!"

Sometimes I think that guy is crazy. But he's big when he's mad, so I didn't say anything. Just when he was ready to go, I said, "You can take that watch with you. I'm just going to be sitting here, anyway."

"Please keep it, Sam. It makes me feel better, even if you don't care. Look, this shouldn't take more than an hour or two. It's a beautiful day. The snow is almost gone. Let's take our bikes over to the canal this afternoon."

"We were supposed to buy my new sneakers this afternoon, if you only remembered," I said.

"Well, we'll do that, too," he said. "We'll have plenty of time to do everything."

I walked out of the room, without looking back.

"You can leave the watch if you want to."

The first thing I did was use up the one hour of television Robbie allowed me every day, and the second thing I did was steal another half hour.

Then I looked in my room, where there was nothing to do, and then in the living room, where there was also nothing to do. I grabbed my jacket and the pocket watch from the table and went downstairs.

The postman was putting mail in the mailboxes. He handed me a postcard. It was from Kristie.

"Fabulous skiing here! Leave for L.A. tomorrow, then home. I cut my hair! Sample: 17 inches! Luv and XXXXXXXXXX!!! K." The sample was one long black hair carefully coiled and taped to the card.

The picture showed a mountain in Colorado with three skiers zooming down. The postmark was from Los Angeles. I thought I might be a lawyer when I grew up. It sounded great.

I heard some familiar sounds from the alley, Picker sounds. That was something good, anyway. I pressed my face against the dirty window in the rear hall door.

Only the High Picker was there. And for once he was not looking for trash. He just seemed to be thinking, thinking hard as he slowly pushed his cart. That High Picker, pushing his baby carriage!

Just opposite my window he stopped and turned, looking for something, waiting for somebody. When he stood so quietly, I noticed his coat was as ragged as the coat of the drunken bum. He put up his hand, to wave, or beckon to someone, or just to feel the air. He put up his hand, and after a moment he brought it down.

The Singing Picker Woman came then, walking as if her feet were sore. Her mouth was moving, but I couldn't hear the song.

She walked up to the High Picker, until she was standing right against him, and she put her arms around him. He wrapped his long arms around her and gave her a long, long kiss, right in my alley.

I wasn't embarrassed, I just watched, and it was okay. I liked to know they loved each other like that.

Even when the Pickers stopped kissing, they didn't start to work right away. They stood close, with their faces close, and talked softly, nodding and nodding. They patted each other on the back in a friendly way.

I wished I knew what they were saying. I wiped a clean place on the glass so I could see better. I wished I knew where the Dog Picker was. I wished I were part of it.

Then the High Picker went to get a pile of papers from across the alley. I had never seen the Pickers take papers before. The woman stood by the wagon just waiting. When he dumped the papers in the wagon, she put her hand on his arm, and they passed slowly down the alley.

I raced for the front steps.

The Pickers came out of the alley slowly, arm in

arm, the man pushing the wagon and watching for cars, the woman staring straight ahead.

I gave them Kristie's thumb sign: Give me a lift, take me with you, I want to go your way. Of course, they didn't notice. I remembered Bob, that golden mustache guy; I took my hand down and pushed it into my pocket.

The Pickers crossed the street. A small ugly collie who lives over there followed them into the next alley, yapping. And then they were really gone.

I took the gold watch out of my pocket. I watched a minute pass, then I put the watch away and sat on the stoop.

The street was empty of people and moving cars. Nothing was happening. The tops of the gingko trees were moving, but there was no wind below, where I was. I wished K'e would come by, but K'e only came when he came.

I hadn't seen Phillip for a long time on a Saturday. Did I get tired of him or did he get tired of me? I tried to remember. It didn't matter.

I wished I could go!

It was wonderful weather for doing something good. It was still winter, but the sun was practicing for spring, melting the snow, and making the air fresh and clear and almost warm. It was a day to do something. I wanted to go away, to where people were doing good things together.

Go! In that sporty yellow car zapping down the

street now, and gone. Wheels! Go! That old Picker wagon, even, helping those Pickers to drag around their stuff.

If I went with the Pickers, around and around, I knew how it could be. I could help them get their junk and listen to them laughing and talking and telling each other the stories and the news. When I got tired, they would let me lie down in their wagon; the Singing Picker Woman would make me a place in the papers and the clothes and the things. I could lie and watch the treetops going by, watch the trees move backwards against the sky. And when the wagon was full and they headed for home, I would lie in the wagon, and they would roll me home, while the Singing Picker Woman sang.

That was one of those dreams that wouldn't be so good—I knew it—if it did come true, but it made me feel good, dreaming.

I put out my thumb again. Just hop on my thumb! I remembered the excitement when Kristie came. It was exciting to arrive. I stepped off the bottom step and walked to the curb, pretending. I wished that little sporty car would come by again. I would go!

"Hey, kid!" A lady in an old blue car was hollering. "You need a ride?"

I smiled. I recognized her—the doughnut lady from the drunken bum's park. She was happy like Kristie; still, she was crazy.

"Come on! I just bought some doughnuts. I'll take

you where you're going. Or we can just eat doughnuts and ride around."

There she was, like magic, exactly when I needed
a ride, exactly when I stuck out my thumb. I knew
for sure, right away, that she was crazy but nice, too.
My father's rule about not getting into cars with
strangers seemed a rule for other people and other
days. I knew what I was doing. I got in.

"Sure," I said. "Thanks."

"Just dump my bag on the floor," she said. I put
her straw pocketbook down carefully. "Aren't you
the kid that was with that other kid in the park?"

I nodded. It was nice she remembered me.

"Hah!" She grinned, then she stepped on the gas
and the car jerked away with a roar that would have
made K'e happy. It sure made me happy.

Right away I felt bad, too. I felt as if Robbie were
standing on the curb, watching and shaking his head,
making me feel bad right when I was feeling so good.

"Where to?" the woman said, reaching out to shake
my hand. "I'm Ellen Eyres."

I shook. "I'm Sam," I said, and I pushed my dumb
Dad right out of my mind.

"Take a doughnut, Sam. Will you take one this
time?"

"Sure. Why not?"

"I'm not a stranger any more! Hah! Take a couple." Ellen Eyres handed me a white bag with grease
spots on it. "They got a new kind, those ones with

powdered sugar and lemon filling. They're lousy. Give
me a chocolate one, will you? Where to?"

"Let's just ride around," I said, copying her easy
way.

I looked into the bag for a long moment. She had
about fifteen doughnuts. She had said a couple, so I
took two, the new kind and a chocolate.

"Like it?" she asked.

I nodded; my mouth was full.

"You eat those. I just bought them because the
man there told me they were new. What I love is
chocolate."

I swallowed my bite. "And doughnuts are pretty
nourishing, too." I was hoping she would offer me
more later.

"Yeah," Ellen Eyres said, but she didn't seem to
be interested in nutrition.

There was something strange about her driving.
I was jerked forward and back when she put on
the brakes too quickly after going too fast toward
a red light. And I swayed from side to side as the car
swayed, because Ellen Eyres didn't steer straight.
She liked to move the steering wheel back and forth
a lot, the way a little kid pretends to drive by wiggling the wheel.

But I didn't care. I was feeling like a star, rushing
through the streets, as fast, finally, as I had ever
wanted to go, and with doughnuts, my third and
fourth, in each hand.

And there was K'e to see me! K'e was riding toward us on his bike, straight down the middle, wrong way down a one-way street. Ellen Eyres swerved and K'e swerved, and they missed each other.

"Crazy kid!" she yelled as we passed him.

"K'e!" I yelled, and held up the doughnuts for him to see as he whizzed by my window.

I hoped K'e had noticed me, being so grand.

10
Crazy Yourself

The car pitched sideways again. Crazy yourself, I was thinking.

Ellen Eyres's hair was all different lengths, in back long enough to stick under her collar, on top short and bristly as a toothbrush. She probably just cut off a piece whenever it got in her way.

"Hah!" she said, about nothing I could see.

I looked at the front part of her head. I could imagine her crazy brains, like blind gray worms, crawling and wiggling and thinking crazy words, and trying to find out something right. Then "Hah!"—one of her crazy ideas would zap them like an electric shock, stiff and still. But in a second they would start again, wriggling and crawling through each other in a tight pile inside her skull.

She wore her glasses on the end of her nose. Instead of pushing them up so she could see better, she tilted her head back to look through them. When she talked to me, her chin pointed out at me like the front end of a jet. I liked it better when she watched the street and talked sideways.

"Okay! Sam, you like dogs?"

"Yeah. Most of them."

"We'll drive around and look at dogs. Lots of dogs out on Saturdays. People have the time to walk them. I like to look at dogs on Saturdays."

"There's one," I said.

"See how the smells pull him along by the nose? All the good smells he couldn't find when things were frozen, getting ripe now the sun is warm. I wish I was a dog. Hah!" She stopped at a red light and looked at me. "You got a dog?"

"No."

"I wish I had one. They won't let me have a dog in my building. Nothing like cuddling a dog."

"I got the same thing," I said. "No dogs allowed."

"Who do you live with? Your parents?"

"My dad." I got ready for the usual question. But all Ellen Eyres said was "Yeah," almost like she knew.

She drove around my neighborhood a little more, then suddenly she stuck out her chin even farther and stepped on the gas. The engine roared. I watched her leaning forward over the wheel; how fierce her eyes were, how sharp her chin was. For the first time I wondered if she could be kidnapping me.

But I had only gotten into her car because I wanted to. And she was very nice. All those doughnuts. And since she didn't make me wear a seat belt, I was freer here than in Robbie's car. Hah! on him. He probably wasn't even home yet.

The back seat of her car was full of junk—newspapers and some fat paper bags and a pair of boots and a sneaker. I thought Ellen Eyres must be poor.

The streets were sliding back and forth behind the rear window. Ellen Eyres was really moving that wheel. For the first time I was not enjoying her driving. All those doughnuts, inside.

There was a McDonald's up ahead. The doughnuts had made me thirsty, and I wished we could stop, but I didn't know what Ellen Eyres would do if I made that suggestion. It didn't exactly worry me that she was crazy, but she might be insulted if I asked for a drink and she was poor. Also, if she was kidnapping me, she might not want to show her face in there. It was better not to ask.

Ellen Eyres parked the car. "Let's get something to drink at McDonald's," she said. Ellen Eyres would make a wonderful mother.

She bought herself a cup of coffee and me a root beer to take out. Robbie Diefenbach was spending the whole dumb Saturday morning talking about healthy food and his kid was out having doughnuts and root beer before lunch. Hah!

Ellen Eyres said her place was nearby and there were more doughnuts there. I didn't exactly need another doughnut for a while, but I was curious about her home. Maybe she lived in low-income housing. Also, as soon as we got there, I would call Dad and let him know where I was.

I took a quick sip of my root beer and raced to catch up with her fast lunging walk, out the door, through an alley, along a wide avenue for a few blocks and into a small apartment building.

"I live on the third floor," she said.

"Me, too."

Ellen Eyres flashed me her big grin. It was nice, making Ellen Eyres happy.

Her building wasn't like ours at all. It was a regular apartment house, but small. There was dirt and trash on the stairs, and a cat complaining. I heard water spilling, as if plumbing had broken somewhere and there was no one home to fix it. And it was dark in there.

In the second-floor hall Ellen Eyres suddenly turned and held her finger to her lips. "Don't say anything!" she hissed. I wasn't talking, but she was so fierce I nodded.

She moved down the dark hall like a sneaking

witch. I followed close. When she came to a certain door, she handed me her coffee and her sack.

She faced the door and jerked her arms above her head. She flicked her wrists, with her fingers straight. Her face was ugly and terrible, as if she could see right through the door, into the face of the person she was hating.

Maybe Ellen Eyres wasn't crazy and nice, I thought. Maybe she was crazy and mean. I moved back two steps. That's when I should have run.

She took a long time hating, wriggling her whole body, jerking her arms, fingers stiff and threatening, bewitching whatever was behind the closed door. Her mouth moved, but I couldn't hear anything. She was all swirling, hot and crazy inside, with her muscles hard, like when I get flaming crazy. But on the outside she wasn't doing anything real. She never even touched the door.

Then her arms fell, and she stood still, staring at the door, watching, I imagined, to be sure the person she hated was dead.

Then she smiled and turned and beckoned for me to come. I came. It wasn't a tricky witch's smile now, but a smile like a friend's. She took back her coffee and had a sip. She giggled, and we ran thumping up the second flight of stairs to her door. She had to unlock three locks with three different keys. She peeked in for a second, then opened the door wide.

"Welcome to my home sweet home!"

I was so surprised and relieved I laughed. And she laughed, and I felt comfortable with her again. I hated some people myself, after all; what was so bad about that?

Ellen Eyres's apartment had two rooms. The first one had two old chairs by a table in the middle. A ceiling bulb and a hanging bulb were the only lights in the room. Ellen Eyres turned them on as soon as we came in. Only the hanging bulb had a shade; it swung on its long cord, making moving shadows on the walls and all around.

Pictures were stuck around the walls and newspapers were stacked high in the corners, with half-full coffee cups on them and open magazines and a hairbrush and makeup and some medicines and candy bar wrappers. Along one wall was a couch, more like a bed, with pillows at one end. Lined up on another wall were a small sink, a small stove, a small refrigerator, and a small cupboard. That room could be the living room, the dining room, the kitchen, or the bedroom.

The other room was almost the same, with the same kind of mess, except there was a television set on the middle table there, and no kitchen. Her apartment was like the waiting room at the bus station, where no one cleaned much.

Ellen Eyres locked the three locks with her three keys.

"There," she said. "You have to be careful. There are some wild people around here. Make yourself at home, Sam."

You could either call Ellen Eyres's apartment a pile of junk, or you could roam around in it and find the good things. The best thing I found was a unicycle.

"Sure, go ahead. Try it. You won't be able to," Ellen Eyres said.

"Can you?"

"I never tried. It was left here by a friend of mine. When he cut out, he left by bus and not by unicycle. Hah!"

"I'm going to try."

"Sure. Start in a corner, and use the walls to balance with." She poured some more milk in her coffee and took a doughnut and went to turn on the TV in the other room.

The unicycle was hard work. And it was hard to concentrate on that when there were other things to investigate. Ellen Eyres didn't seem to mind that I wandered around, touching and trying whatever I liked.

After a while I looked into the refrigerator, then in the cupboard. I was getting hungry, but everything she had made me feel sick just to think about: doughnuts and sodas, stuff like that.

I wanted to just say, "It's time for me to go home now." I practiced, inside, as if I were just going to say it out loud, just say it. But I didn't know what she would do.

I remembered that I had planned to call my dad. That would be easier. I looked around, but I didn't see a phone. I went to the door of the other room and let my eyes get used to the dimness there. The only thing I could see well was Ellen Eyres's face, full of television light. I watched her awhile, watching her watching television the same way she drove, with her head tilted back so she could see through the glasses on the end of her nose. I watched her, and I thought about what I would say to my father. I would have to say where I was, and explain how I got there. And he was already mad, I knew it, from finding no note. Calling him wouldn't be easy, after all.

Without planning to, I asked her, "Miss Eyres, are you kidnapping me?"

"Hah!" she said. "Call me Ellen." After a minute she asked, "Don't you like it here?"

"I like it, but I miss my dad a little. I wish I could call him." I waited for her to offer me the phone. She didn't. "I'm supposed to call him if I go to someone's house," I said. Robbie's rules sounded silly, said to Ellen Eyres.

After a long wait she said, "If you called him, he'd probably want you to come home."

That idea sounded nice, my dad wanting me home, coming to get me in our own car, driving home together, and fixing me a grilled cheese and a blended OJ on ice.

But the way Ellen Eyres said it, not looking at me and a little fierce, reminded me that she was crazy. I didn't answer.

The next thing she said was, "Don't you miss your mom, too? Is she dead, or did she cut out?"

"My mom and dad are divorced."

"That's the way, isn't it, honey? So many people gone! It makes you lonely. I bet!" She lit a cigarette, and blew a long stream of smoke right at me. "You can stay here awhile, Sam. I don't have anybody. Someone cut out on me, too. And no dogs allowed. Hah! You can't trust anybody." Her voice was angry, then kind. "I'll be glad to have you."

She seemed to think I needed a home and a friend. She didn't even notice about my father. I had my father. I almost screamed it at her: "I'm not lonely!" I didn't need her; I had Dad. I wanted to say it. "It's time for me to go home now," but it didn't seem to fit into our conversation.

She gave me a warm smile, which made me shiver. She got up suddenly and made another cup of coffee. I watched her pour in her milk and slam and bang the refrigerator door and slam the pot into the sink.

Her smile was true, but so was her slamming and banging. A numb fright was taking over my body. One minute I would be sure my father was coming to get me, and the next minute I would be sure he couldn't possibly find me. I wondered if Phillip would remember about meeting Ellen Eyres and tell Dad. I wondered if she had kidnapped me and if Dad really didn't have enough money to get me back.

I sat down and listened to the television noise from the other room.

11
The Lonesome Guest

Late Saturday afternoon Ellen Eyres cooked our supper: a can of chicken noodle soup, a can of cheese ravioli, and no vegetables. Also, we made a package of strawberry Jell-O and divided it into two big bowls. We took turns spraying on the whipped topping, passing the can back and forth, to keep it fair, piling it higher and higher, until we had used it all.

After supper Ellen Eyres watched television, and I mostly wandered around. I didn't like her shows much. I tried the unicycle some more, but I couldn't work it. I knew her apartment too well now; I couldn't find anything to do.

I got so bored I was brave enough to ask, "May I use your phone?"

"They took it," Ellen Eyres said, sucking deep on her cigarette. The smoke rose from the edges of her mouth and melted into the light of the bulb over her head.

I looked around. There was no phone in that room, either. It seemed dangerous to be in a house with no telephone.

"They took it, and now they can't call me about it any more, the pissers!" Ellen Eyres drew quick breaths, letting out little round puffs of smoke, playing with it, shaping it, pushing the puffs into the light. I could have been hypnotized watching the smoke shapes, but my ears had heard that wonderful word.

"Pissers," I said.

"Pissers! Pissers, pissers!" said Ellen Eyres. Suddenly she wasn't angry, she was giggling with me. "They are!"

She ran into the other room and cleared the table, slamming her dish and her bowl into the sink. They didn't break, but she didn't wash them. She sounded angry again.

I followed her in. I felt safer keeping an eye on her when she was angry; also, I enjoyed the rumpus.

She saw me smiling and gave a happy shriek. She ran to the window, jerked it open, and shouted out into the chill air, "Pissers!"

The word echoed up the alley walls, but Ellen Eyres wanted something else.

"Pisssssssers!" she yelled, and stamped on the floor. She yelled it three or four times again, with the same high screaming energy; each time, she stamped on the floor.

She got her answer. The person in the apartment below knocked on his ceiling in sharp, angry knocks. I was afraid then, more afraid of knocks by an unknown person than of Ellen Eyres's angry, merry screams.

"Ah!" she whispered. "That's him." She yelled, "Pissers!" one last time, to show she paid no attention to such knocks, and slammed down the window. "Do you play gin?" she asked.

I didn't, but she taught me. We played for hours, drinking sodas, sometimes stopping to look at the television she kept going in the other room. Ellen Eyres popped hunks of smoke into the light. We didn't talk much, but we both played hard and we had some good games. I taught her how to play "Fish," too, and she liked it okay, but "Gin!" she yelled as soon as I beat her. "Gin, you pisser!" So we went back to gin.

"I used to play a lot of gin," Ellen Eyres said. After a while she asked, "Do you miss your momma, Sam?"

"Well, but I always miss her." That wasn't really what I meant. Now that I knew Ellen Eyres and liked

her, I didn't mind her asking about Sheila. I wanted
to give her a true answer, but what was true? "Well,
I don't exactly miss her," I said finally. "I miss something. . . ."

"It's hard, isn't it? Gone! You get so damned mad."

"Yeah. But sometimes I just forget about her."
Forget about my own mother! I had never said that
before, even to myself, but that was true.

"Well, sure. She cut out, didn't she? Forget her!"

"It's not that I miss Sheila so much. I miss having
a mother." I was glad to understand that, to know
how I felt. "It's not having a mother at all that I
miss. I'm angry at Sheila that she went away and I
can't have a mother."

"Yeah," Ellen Eyres said. "Yeah," she said. "Yeah."
That was all we said about it.

And then I was so sleepy I couldn't focus my eyes
on the cards. Ellen Eyres went into the other room
and pushed some things off the couch onto the floor
to make a place for me. She didn't remind me to take
off my clothes, even my sneakers. She didn't say I
should wash my face or brush my teeth. It was wonderful to be so sleepy and be able to just lie down
and go to sleep. Ellen Eyres plumped my pillow and
brought a heavy gray blanket from the other room
to cover me and turned off the television set.

"Good night, Sam. You're a fabulous gin player.
We'll have fun tomorrow, too."

"Thank you," I said, just like I was a guest, just like this was a usual visit. "Good night."

As Ellen Eyres was going out the door, I got terribly lonely. Maybe because she was talking about tomorrow, reminding me that I would wake up at her home, not at mine. "I wish I could call my dad and tell him I'm here," I said.

"I know your daddy, honey. I told him you were here," Ellen Eyres said, kindly. "Go to sleep." She went into the other room.

I couldn't remember when in the whole confusing day she might have told Robbie. But I was not surprised that he knew Ellen Eyres. Often when he and I were out walking, we would pass someone who would say "Hi" to him and Dad would say "Hi" back. I would wait until the person was gone and then ask, "Do you really know him?" or "What's her name?" Robbie always knew those other people. That was another thing about him.

Suddenly I realized when Ellen Eyres might have talked to Robbie: when she called him with the kidnap message! Then he knew. And he hadn't come to get me.

I flipped myself around on the couch as if I could flip my way out of there. I hated it all!

But there was something uncomfortable; some way I couldn't lie right. I was lying on top of Robbie's watch. I pulled it out of my pocket. It was seven minutes past twelve midnight, and he hadn't come.

I rubbed the soft warm gold. I wished I had left the watch at home; maybe he would have sold it to get the money to get me back.

I put the watch under my ear so I could hear the ticking. If you have a new baby puppy and he's lonely in the night, you should wrap a wind-up clock up in a towel and put that close by him. The ticking reminds him of his mother's heart beating, and he doesn't feel so sad. I was feeling like that lonesome puppy, and Robbie's watch ticking made me not so sad and lonely, so I could cry just softly, to myself. I moved the watch a little, so it wouldn't get wet. Always leaving the watch was a good thing about my dad.

I went to sleep holding the watch tightly, in case Ellen Eyres turned out to be a robber, too.

12
The Strongest Lock That Ever Was

I was awake long before Ellen Eyres.

For breakfast there were doughnuts. Even before my first bite I could tell they were stale. I ate a few pieces, but they tasted like heavy powder. I swallowed hard, but my throat felt all stuffed up with doughnut glue.

I opened the refrigerator, wanting some juice or a piece of fruit, a carrot, even. I used to think everyone kept juice around, like I used to think everyone had a phone. The only thing Ellen Eyres had that might taste good was some milk. I drank it right up from the carton and threw the carton away. My throat felt better, but my stomach didn't. I wasn't hungry, just not satisfied, from eating old food. I wished I had one of those big co-op grapefruit. I wished my dad hadn't taught me all that health stuff and made my mouth taste so bad.

I had nothing to do. The gray light, which seemed to come not from a yellow sun but directly from the greasy windows, put a deadness on everything. There was no sound. It was as if we were on an island, and there was nothing else, just Ellen Eyres, sleeping, and me. I walked around the room.

Ellen Eyres had slept in a chair, not on the couch. Her blanket fell crookedly across her body, and she snored slightly. Her snoring was like a little kid whining. She looked boring and not pretty, and I stopped looking at her.

I wanted to go home. I tried not to think about why Dad hadn't come. All I knew for sure was I would have to do something myself.

Very quietly I tried the front door. The three locks were locked. I didn't see her straw bag with the keys anywhere.

A bit of color showed from one of the newspaper piles. I pulled out an old Sunday comics section. It was one I hadn't read. I tumbled black-and-white sections on the floor and read months and months of Sunday comics.

I had forgotten about Ellen Eyres, and when she

snorted and moved, I was startled. I thought she might be angry that I had messed up her piles. But she just sat on the edge of her chair, waiting to stand up, looking at me, not smiling, not angry, just looking.

I didn't want to say something until she said something. I couldn't remember what kinds of things we said to each other. I pretended to read.

"Did you eat?" she asked.

"The doughnuts are stale."

"I buy them day-old. Cheap."

"Do you have any juice?"

"Hah! Fancy!"

She went to the stove and put on water to heat. She took the top off the coffee jar, and opened the refrigerator. As soon as I heard that door open, I knew I had made a mistake.

"Pisser!" she hissed at me. "Milk!" she shouted. "Milk!" She grabbed the empty carton from the trash and held it up. "You are never to finish the milk without my permission. Never, ever again!"

She threw the carton at me, hard. It didn't hurt.

She slammed the pot with the hot water into the sink and grabbed a handful of doughnut pieces and jammed them into her mouth. Crumbs fell behind her as she stomped into the other room.

When I heard the television, I figured I was safe for a while. I was frightened, not by her throwing the carton or even the screaming, but by those words, "Never, ever again." I was trapped with Ellen Eyres, forever.

I could see her face, staring into the television light. I wished that TV could jump onto Ellen Eyres's lap and spin its long antennas both ways in fast circles around her neck. Then I could make my getaway!

I tried to make myself think of a plan. I tried to make my brain think of something I could really do.

If you were in danger, you were supposed to yell and make a lot of noise to attract attention. But if I banged on the floor and yelled out the window, the neighbors would just think it was crazy Ellen Eyres being crazy again. They wouldn't pay attention.

And Ellen Eyres would grab me.

The door was locked. Yelling wouldn't work. And there was no phone. I had to figure out some other way to get myself out of there.

So I planned, and I did one of the hardest things I had ever done. I made someone else do something I needed her to do, without asking her, without even letting her know what I wanted. I made Ellen Eyres unlock her three locks and take me outside.

I went into the other room. I watched her for a moment to be sure her anger had stopped, and then I went near. I waited until there was a commercial. Then I said: "I'm sorry I drank your milk. Would you like me to get you another doughnut?"

Ellen Eyres patted my back and said she would. I brought it.

"They're stale," I said, careful not to insult her housekeeping, but to show I was sorry her breakfast wasn't very good. "That was the last big piece." I had hidden the others in the trash.

"Two people eat a lot more doughnuts than one does, Sam." Her voice was pretty friendly.

"I guess so," I said.

"You like doughnuts, don't you?"

"I love doughnuts, especially chocolate," I said. I remembered she especially liked chocolate. Then I said, very carefully, very kindly, "I'm sorry I drank your milk, so you can't have coffee with your doughnuts."

"Don't worry, Sam. We can go buy more. As soon as this program's done, we'll go. The store's not far."

That was what I had been waiting for. Quietly I went back to the other room. I didn't dare say anything else; my voice might sound so happy she would guess my plan.

She took a long time getting ready to leave. She watched another program. Then I heard the window slam open. She had heard something I hadn't. Someone coming to rescue me? I ran in.

"I'll be calling! I'll call them tomorrow," Ellen Eyres was yelling out the window. "They'll be coming for you!"

I couldn't see anything, anyone at all. It could

mean anything. She was screaming now, screaming and pausing and screaming again. I went back into the other room and waited. I had heard her scream before.

I waited more than half an hour. Once I slammed the refrigerator door to remind her that she wanted milk for a nice cup of coffee. Mostly I was imagining how I would get away once we were outside.

At last she came in. "I'm going to the store."

Carefully, casually, I put on my jacket. "Can we get doughnuts, too?" I asked. I was asking about the doughnuts, but what I cared about was the "we." I was afraid she might change her mind and lock me up behind.

"Sure!" she said. "You like doughnuts, don't you? I never saw a kid eat so many doughnuts."

"I love them." I smiled, although my mouth ached at the idea of eating any more doughnuts. I was lying, but I had to, to get out of the crazy, messy apartment, which was making me almost dizzy now.

Ellen Eyres couldn't find her shoes, then she couldn't find her scarf. I found them for her.

"Ooooo-eee, you *are* a help!" she said. "I like having you around."

I made my mouth smile again, hoping she couldn't tell my smile was a lie. I tried to remember if I had forgotten anything, in case I never came back. My father's watch was in my pocket.

Ellen Eyres jangled her key ring with the many

keys on it, and fussed and cursed and got the three locks undone. I wondered what all the other keys were for. Maybe her closets were full of locked boxes full of crazy secrets.

My body was tense and trembling as I waited for her to open the door. I had been locked up in that apartment for almost twenty-four hours. When I stepped out into the dark hall, for the first time in my life I knew what freedom meant. I felt a rush of power in my body. As soon as we got outdoors, I would run like crazy.

But my freedom lasted only that moment. As soon as Ellen Eyres had locked the three locks and turned and looked at me, it was as if she could see right through my eyes into my head and know my plans. Her hard eyes were on me like when she was witching that man right through his door. She grabbed hold of my wrist, like the strongest, hardest lock that ever was.

And she didn't let go. Her hand burned, twisting tight around my wrist, and forced us to go down the stairs in a close and awkward way. When Ellen Eyres didn't let go then, I knew she meant to keep hold of me every minute until we were in her apartment again.

My stomach tightened and heaved. I thought I might throw up, thinking about going back to the prison upstairs.

"Are you cold, honey?" Ellen Eyres asked, and her

voice was kind. "It's still not spring, is it? I should knit you a pretty red sweater one of these days. I like a boy in a red sweater."

I didn't want her to talk about "one of these days." I didn't want it!

And it hurt, being held like that. My arm itched. I just wanted to be able to move my own arm. I pulled on my arm inside her hand. I did not get free.

"Any kid who wants a red sweater," Ellen Eyres said, "better behave." She pulled my hand back up that uncomfortable way. And she held it up there as we walked the four long blocks to the supermarket.

I had planned to run, but the pain in my wrist was a warning: if I tried to get away, Ellen Eyres would squeeze her tight witch's hold until only a skinny bit of skin was wrapped around my wrist bone. She would squeeze until my hand dropped off dead in the street.

13
Day-Old Doughnuts

Ellen Eyres's strong grip didn't loosen once we were in the store. She made me help push the cart. We each had one hand on the cart handle; her other hand held my wrist. I picked the food she wanted from my side of the aisle, and she picked the food from her side. Up and down the aisles we went, always together.

When we first came into the store, while Ellen Eyres was choosing three boxes of day-old doughnuts, I noticed a tall man unpacking food, helping people, moving around. I knew this strong man would be the best person to help me. As we came to the end of each aisle, I would look back and forth, trying to find him. I saw him only a few times, and each time we moved the other way. I realized that Ellen Eyres had seen him, too.

Even if I did get close to that man, I was no longer sure I would have the courage to try to get away. If I complained to him, why should he believe me? He might just kick us both out of the store, and she would take me back to the apartment and lock me up forever. It took all the courage I had not to let my tears fall out.

Finally the store music and the slow walking and going by all the familiar brands and boxes and cans began to calm me down. Ellen Eyres was not a good shopper: she passed slowly down each aisle three or four times, with no particular plan, never taking much. She began to relax, too, and she was fun to shop with; for a little while she was like my old friend again.

Many times in my life I had wanted to stand in front of the cereal shelves and the cookie shelves and think about whether I liked or I didn't like every single kind. Ellen Eyres was the first grown-up I ever met who liked to do that. She asked which cookies I liked best. I thought a long time, and when I couldn't decide between two, she flipped both boxes into the cart.

"How do you have enough money?" I asked. I had never seen anyone shop that way, not choosing, taking both.

"I don't, I don't!" she said, laughing. She looked deep into her bag. "Maybe I have enough. Or maybe I'll get a letter tomorrow, and we can buy more then."

"Tomorrow." The word rang in my head, reminding me of my danger. In a second my body was empty of the calm feeling, and I slowly, slowly began to fill with a trembling courage.

When she asked what cereal I liked, and she took the giant size, breakfast for tomorrow, and the next day, and the next, I looked desperately for the tall man. He passed across the end of our aisle, heading toward the dairy section.

"Shouldn't we get the milk?" I asked.

"For my precious coffee! Hah!" Ellen Eyres led me to the dairy aisle and picked a quart of milk. "Now I want you to drink a glass of this as soon as we get home," she said sternly. I couldn't see why she was so serious; I loved milk.

The tall man was not in sight. The bright row of fruits and vegetables opposite the dairy cases looked cool and moist and crisp and fresh. My mouth ached for a bite of something that wasn't soft or dry or sugary or stale.

My hand shot out; I had green grapes in my mouth in a second. They were more delicious than any food

119

I had ever tasted. I closed my eyes, and let my whole body be my mouth.

But Ellen Eyres suddenly jerked my wrist over close to her. My eyes flashed open. The tall man stood right there watching me. His eyes looked into my eyes, and I knew that this was my chance.

Slowly and deliberately, I reached over and took an apple. Noisily I bit a large chunk. I chewed slowly, then I took another loud bite.

The tall man smiled slightly and shook his head, more to himself than to me. I was afraid Ellen Eyres might just walk me right by him, away. To make him do something, I quickly put the apple behind my back.

"Lady, your kid took some fruit," the man said, not angry, just annoyed.

Ellen Eyres's grip was like a trap now. She let go of the shopping cart and pulled me back a step.

"Why'd you take that apple?" she asked harshly. She slapped it out of my hand, and it rolled across the floor, picking up dirt on the wet white parts where I had bitten.

My hand stung. I was surprised that my heart stung, too, because Ellen Eyres had slapped me.

"You'll have to pay for that," the tall man said. "Tell them at the checkout. Go pick it up, kid."

The grip on my hand loosened, but only a little. Ellen Eyres didn't want to let me go.

"I'm not her kid," I said to the tall man. "She took me."

"Shut up," Ellen Eyres whispered fiercely.

The tall man watched us closely now. "Let him pick up the apple, lady."

"The fresh kid," she mumbled. She couldn't seem to make herself look at the tall man; she couldn't seem to make herself let go of my wrist.

"Let me go, Miss Eyres." I said it slowly and loudly so the tall man would have no doubt about what she was doing. Other shoppers were watching now. I needed them to hear, too, no matter how stupid it sounded or how embarrassed I was to have everyone staring at me. I looked Ellen Eyres in the eye. "Let me go!"

Then she did let go. She swung my arm back, and then flung it forward so fast I hit myself. A dirty trick, a little kid's trick. Ellen Eyres laughed. I staggered backward. I was free.

I could feel the blood rushing into my tingling hand. I checked the tall man, for a second, before I went to get the apple. I wanted to be sure nothing would happen when I turned my back on Ellen Eyres.

As I walked, I could feel the distance between us growing like a fresh wind. The farther I got from her, the smaller she looked.

I brought the apple back, but I stopped before I got near Ellen Eyres, so she stayed small. I could see her hand and her fingers gesturing for me to come near, trying to get her grip on me again. I threw the apple into the cart, and again I said to the tall man, "She took me. I'm not her kid."

"Pisser!" Ellen Eyres stomped closer, so the ugly breath of the word hissed in my ear and made me shiver. That woman was crazy.

"Damn the kid! I'm his aunt," she told the tall man.

"What's your name?" the man asked me.

A panic flashed across Ellen Eyres's eyes. "His name is Sam Eyres," she said quickly.

Sam Eyres!

The tall man heard me gasp. "What's your name, son?" he asked again, more kindly this time. But I couldn't take my eyes from Ellen Eyres. She was moving her hands in and out, up and down, flexing her fingers, moving them through the air like a cat ready to pounce. I couldn't answer until the man stepped between us. If she pounces now, I thought, she'll land on him.

"My name is Sam Diefenbach," I said. The sound of my real name, my dad's name, made me feel surer. Ellen Eyres's hands pounced, helplessly, up in the air, and down again.

"Where do you live?" the man asked.

I gave my address.

"What's your father's name? I'll call."

"Robbie Diefen. . ." I started.

"Robbie!" Ellen Eyres screamed. "Robbie! His father's name is Robbie. Don't you think I know that? Cut out and left. Gone! Left the kid with Ellen. Didn't I treat you well, Sam? Supper and everything? Didn't we have fun?"

"She treated me well," I said, trying to be fair. I couldn't look at her, though. I could only look at the tall man. "My father's name is Robbie Diefenbach. I can tell you the phone number."

"Robbie Diefenbach!" Ellen Eyres was screaming so desperately I almost wished her lies were true, for her sake. "Robbie Diefenbach! Don't you think I know!"

She began digging frantically into the cart, pulling the doughnuts from their boxes and throwing them at me. I didn't even try to duck. Doughnuts don't hurt. I stood there letting her hit me with doughnuts, hearing her screams, watching her, hating her, hating Ellen Eyres, ashamed for her and for myself.

"Damn kid!" she yelled. "Pissers! Gone! Left Ellen. Cut out! Gone! Stop looking at me!" She started throwing the doughnuts at the people who stood watching her craziness growing, swelling up inside her, leaking out with doughnut crumbs all over the supermarket floor.

Beyond my tears, I heard a new sound. I blinked and saw two policemen wrestling with her. Her

123

glasses fell off the end of her nose onto the floor.
And I saw Dad running with his arms wide open
to gather me in.

14
Beautiful
Evidence

My father's hand was not like Ellen Eyres's hand. My father's hand held my hand gently; it didn't try to keep me.

We were sitting in the back of a police car parked in front of the store, waiting to be taken home. Dad told me how scared he had been for me, how he had called the police but nobody had any clues.

"Then how did you find me?" I asked.

"Your friend K'e."

"K'e!"

He told me how K'e had come, how K'e had drawn the evidence, hardly saying a word, putting in his

125

picture everything about how I had gone with Ellen Eyres. Dad told me how long his night had been after that, knowing I had gone off with a stranger woman, waiting scared all night long while the police tried to find the car. They had found the old blue car just an hour before, parked by the McDonald's. He had gone with the police to Ellen Eyres's apartment, but no one was there. The janitor told them to look for her in the supermarket. Dad told me how he had followed the policemen into the store and heard her crazy voice screaming his name.

He gave me another hug. Over his shoulder, out the back window, I saw the police taking Ellen Eyres to another police car. The policemen were not touching her now. She walked between them quietly, her head high, with her glasses back on her nose. Her eyes looked straight ahead and her chin pointed out, as if she knew where she was going and wanted to go there. I was glad they were taking her to jail.

"Did you know her, Dad?"

"No. I never saw her before." That had been another one of her lies.

"I wonder if they'll keep her in jail."

"She committed a crime, son."

"You know, I did it, Dad. I got in her car. I wanted to. It was dumb."

Robbie was very surprised. "Yes. Dumb."

"I think I had the crazies, like Kristie said that time."

But he didn't get mad. He was still loving me an awful lot, and he didn't ask why yet. He just said, "Sam, we all do dumb things. What's important is to recognize it, and to get yourself out of the hole you've gotten yourself into."

"Yeah," I said. "I did that." I sat up tall beside my father. "I used my brain, and I really did it. Not pretend, but with a real kidnapper. I got myself out." But he had come to get me, too. I wanted to remember that part. "Dad? You and I were both trying, the whole time, both of us, to get back together, and we both did it."

My father gave me another hug.

Dad and I went biking the next Saturday. He asked if I would like to invite K'e along, as a way of thanking him for his help.

"Sure! Well, but, Dad? We'd better go on the Canal path. I don't think there's any traffic laws he can break there."

Dad called Mrs. White and got K'e's phone number, so K'e did have a phone. And he spoke to K'e's mother, so K'e did have a mother. And she spoke English, enough anyway, and she said K'e could come. So K'e was not so mysterious any more. Now I knew how to reach him on Saturdays.

And on our bike trip he started talking to us more, and that was better, too. I liked his pictures, but talking is useful, for a friend.

We brought a picnic lunch, and we went seventeen miles round trip. While we ate, Dad asked K'e how he had known I was in danger when I looked so happy in Ellen Eyres's car.

K'e wiggled his hand, like a fish. "Crazy driver," he said. "No good for you." He pointed at Robbie.

Robbie laughed. "You're absolutely right, K'e. I would never let Sam go off with a crazy driver."

"You sure wouldn't," I said. I liked it now, that my father took such careful care of me. "Hey, Dad. Tell me that whole story again, about how K'e drew the picture."

Robbie nodded. "When you didn't come home, Sam, I was more scared than I have ever been."

"And you were mad, too, weren't you, because I didn't leave a note?" He didn't say anything. "I bet you were," I said.

"Yes," he said. "I was mad, at first, before I got so scared. And then I called the police, and when I finally got them interested and they came over, I realized I had very little to tell them, and that scared me even worse. We were sitting around the kitchen table, with no leads at all, when K'e knocked on the door."

"Tah, tah!" I said.

K'e was nodding and nodding.

"He started drawing right away, fast, but carefully, a picture of the car. It was excellent; you could tell the make and the year. The police said it was one of the best eyewitness accounts they had ever had."

"Blue," K'e said.

"Oh, right," Dad said. "He went to your room and found your crayons, and colored the car blue, so they knew the color, too."

"Excellent picture," K'e said, nodding seriously.

"The police were pleased, but I was going crazy— what did that have to do with Sam? And when K'e turned to me and did that same thing"—my dad made the wiggly fish movement with his hand—"and said, 'Crazy driver,' that made me feel even worse."

"That's what Ellen Eyres said about *you*, K'e!" I told him. "She said you were a crazy kid." He grinned. He likes his reputation.

Dad went on. "K'e drew you in there, waving two doughnuts, and with a big smile on your face. I was really upset because I couldn't understand why you were so happy, driving away. And who was the driver?

"Then the policemen started with their questions. How could I tell that was my son when K'e had drawn all that hair over his face? they wanted to know. 'I know it's my son *because* there's hair all over his face,' I said."

K'e laughed and pointed at me.

"Then they asked where he had seen the car. And K'e drew that building with the strange statues embedded in the front, so we all knew it was Corcoran Street. 'That kid can draw!' one of the policemen said."

"Time," K'e said.

"Oh, right," Dad said. "Then the other policeman said, 'Can you tell us what time it was?' He said it like a challenge, didn't he, K'e? Put that in your drawing, if you can! But K'e did it. He drew the postman coming out of the building, and the policeman practically yelled, as if he was the one who had done something clever, 'Great! We'll find out what time the postman was making deliveries on Corcoran.'

"And then it happened," Robbie said, his voice turned very low and serious. "The policemen started to talk to each other, planning what to do next, and I was listening to them. No one was keeping an eye on K'e..."

K'e was laughing, now, waiting to hear the good part.

"...and there on the sidewalk beside the car suddenly appeared this powerful, bare-chested wrestler, with a dark beard and dark glasses, making fierce gestures at the kidnapper's car. And the helpful little arrow and the sign, 'Mrs. Diefenbach.' Well, the policemen were looking at me very strangely, let me tell you, because by now they believed everything K'e drew, and one of them said, 'Were you there?'

and I had to do some very fast explaining about what kind of artist K'e usually is."

"Artist," I heard K'e say to himself.

"I told the policemen about his drawings and pointed out the great white refrigerator shark, and then we looked down, and darned if K'e hadn't put a shark in this picture, too! A shark, swimming underneath Corcoran Street, with its eye on the car, and its mouth opening for a bite of the tires."

"I wish a shark had been there," I said.

K'e nodded and said, "Very beautiful picture, yeah."

"Beautiful, yeah," Dad said. "But then I had to take it away from you pretty quick before you stuck me in there again as a diver, knifing the shark, and those policemen got totally confused. I was lucky I didn't get jailed on suspicion of kidnapping my own son!"

"Where is this picture?" K'e asked.

"The police still have it, I guess," Robbie said. "Would you like me to see if I can get it from them?"

K'e nodded. "Give it to him." He pointed at me. "Tell him to keep safe." He laughed.

"Get it, Dad!" I said.

"I'll try," Robbie said. "They may need to keep it as evidence."

"Very beautiful evidence," K'e said.

When we started to get on the bikes, Robbie noticed, again. "Sam, those sneakers are a wreck."

"Yeah, I need new ones, remember?"

"Weren't we planning to get you new ones?" He looked puzzled, as if he were flipping through his brain pad and couldn't find the right page.

"Yeah. That weekend, last weekend, last Saturday...."

"Oh," he said, and shook his head. "How about we stop at Sears on our way home today and pick up a pair? Those are a disaster."

The last thing Dad did, before we dropped K'e off at his house, was to teach K'e the difference between "Mr." and "Mrs." That was a good day for us all.

15
Too Much Hugging

The next day Robbie had a talk with me, one of those talks where he's checking off items on the brain pad. We were in the car, so his eyes were watching the road, and I was looking out the side window. We weren't looking at each other, and we said what we meant.

He said he had thought for a long time about why a sensible kid like me would get into Ellen Eyres's car.

"Sam, I know it's hard for you not having your mother around. It's hard for me, too. But that's our situation. So. I'll do my best to bring work home.

But I will have to work some Saturdays. I won't ever leave you for long, Sam. I promise you that." When he stopped at a light, he gave me a big hug. "We're okay, Sam. As okay as anybody can be."

After a while he asked, "Would you like to visit Sheila sometime, Sam?"

"I don't know," I said. "I don't know her much. Sheila always says to come visit her, but she never says exactly the day I should come. Maybe I could go there sometime when Kristie goes. I love Kristie."

I remembered talking with Ellen Eyres about not having a mother. I remembered it was Ellen Eyres who helped me the first time I let myself know that it wasn't that I missed Sheila so much; it was more that I was mad at her for leaving me. Ellen Eyres lied a lot, and she tricked me badly, and she kept me, but she was the only person who helped me figure out what I really did feel. Not Robbie, not Kristie, not Phillip even, whose own parents were divorced. I remembered how peaceful I had felt that night after telling the truth to Ellen Eyres.

"Why did Ellen Eyres keep me, Dad? Did she ask you for money for me?"

"No."

"What would you have done if she did want money?"

"I don't know, Sam, but I do know that I would have gotten you back." He looked over at me. "Sam, are you still worried that we're poor?"

"Well. Aren't you?"

"I guess everyone worries about money, some. But I've told you a thousand times, we're okay."

"Okay. Okay, Dad, I knew you'd get me back even if we were poor. But I don't think she meant to kidnap me. We were just going for a ride. And then things changed." I tried to remember how it had happened. "Somebody left her, too, and she was lonely. Like you used to leave me too much."

I began to feel that something was missing between me and Ellen Eyres, maybe just saying goodbye. I asked what had happened to her.

Dad said she was in a hospital now, not in jail. "She's pretty sick, son."

"Crazy?"

"Yes."

"Are they going to help her?"

"Sure," Dad said. "Sure. There are doctors." He looked over and saw my worried face. "Sam? She couldn't live very well by herself now. She doesn't take good care of herself, and she just gets angry at the world when things don't go right."

"Pissers!" I said softly, hissing the s's.

"What?!!!"

"Nothing," I said.

A few weeks later Dad gave me K'e's picture of the kidnapping. I couldn't believe it, me showing the doughnuts and smiling.

135

"We were going to have such a good time," I said.

On the important wall, just above my bed, next to my mom's alligators, I put K'e's picture of me and Ellen Eyres and the shark coming up under Corcoran Street, reminding me to "keep safe."

Dad said they had told him at the police station that Ellen Eyres had been moved from the hospital to her family's home in Boston.

"That's good, Dad! She has a family! She didn't belong to anyone before. There was no one left to miss her when she didn't come home."

Dad started to hug me, but I pushed him away.

"Dad, I hate to tell you, but sometimes there's too much hugging going on around here. You've been hugging me a thousand times. And listen, Dad," I said quickly because he was starting to smile. "Listen! I have to ask you something. Do you think I could do something to help Ellen Eyres?"

He thought for a while, and then he said, "Just staying on with her family will be the best help for her right now, I hope. She needs love, and love takes a lot of time."

"Yeah," I said. "Love takes every Saturday, all day long." I shook my fist at him. "Pow!" I said, and my father and I laughed together. And I let him hug me, one more time.

ABOUT THE AUTHOR

JUDY K. MORRIS started writing for children while working with The Smithsonian Puppet Theater. She turned one of her puppet plays into a story and has been writing children's fiction ever since. She also works as a volunteer teacher of writing in a Washington, D. C., elementary school.

Judy Morris grew up in New York City and was graduated from Swarthmore College. She lives with her husband and their son and daughter in the Dupont Circle area of Washington, D. C., where *The Crazies & Sam* takes place. This is her first book.